Nathaniel L Holmes

An Illustrated City Directory of Hillsdale, Michigan

Nathaniel L Holmes

An Illustrated City Directory of Hillsdale, Michigan

ISBN/EAN: 9783337327385

Printed in Europe, USA, Canada, Australia, Japan

Cover: Foto ©Andreas Hilbeck / pixelio.de

More available books at **www.hansebooks.com**

AN ILLUSTRATED

✼ City Directory ✼

—— OF ——

HILLSDALE, MICHIGAN.

1894.

COMPILED AND PUBLISHED BY

Nathaniel L. Holmes.

ISSUED FROM THE

DEMOCRAT JOB ROOMS,

HILLSDALE.

PUBLISHER'S NOTE.

In putting forth this directory of Hillsdale the fact is fully realized that the work is in a measure, imperfect; the changing of residences in the city, the removing of some from the place as well as others taking up their abode within its limits, all of these constant movements make it impossible for a directory of this place, as of any other, to be absolutely correct in its directing ability.

The Illustrated City Directory of Hillsdale, however, is in the opinion of many who have expressed judgment, practically correct; the list of additions and corrections help in making the work more complete, there being some errors in the general list that have been corrected under this head.

If there are any serious errors, they have crept in almost unavoidably; the publisher sincerely hopes that none of these will be discovered until all collections have been made and he has departed for other points.

Aside from the city directory proper, there have been inserted sketches, in some instances, illustrated. This feature of the work may not at the very present be especially valuable. Yet as time wears on and the ranks of the professional and business men change, these illustrations and portraits will prove to be relics of a very interesting nature. Therefore, combining the two parts, the illustrated and directory, one will be valuable at first and for a short time in directing the public and by the time this feature has become useless, time will have rendered the illus. trations peculiarly attractive and valuable. Thus will this work be for some time to come, an interesting if not particularly a valuable one.

THE PUBLISHER.

August 20, 1894.

P. S.—Owing to the constant changes taking place among residents, an extra sheet will be issued later, probably by September 20, 1894, giving all the latest changes in the city's populace as well as the locations of students during the year '94-95.

The price of this *addenda* will be 50 cents.

THE CITY OF HILLSDALE.

To give anything like a complete historical article on the development of Hillsdale would require space many times the size of a volume such as this; and to undertake it would be practically impossible in this work whose main feature is merely that of a directory, rather than a historical write-up.

The apology offered for inserting it is not that it is the first and original nor that it fills a long felt want in any manner whatever; for the facts have been related heretofore in various articles and publications and in this respect have already become well familiarized; but owing to its concise and limited review of the several industries, business pursuits and professions of the place, with their particular historical data given, it becomes a story giving more completeness to the publication. And perhaps by the way of presenting the facts, it may lend to the subscribers some information worthy of memorization and a better (historically speaking) idea of this very good city of Hillsdale.

The city in size comprises about six square miles, its location being upon what was once a heavy timbered forest; within its limits lies the rising head of the St. Joseph river; the natural water supply lies in a bed of gravel from twenty to sixty feet deep.

Hillsdale long years ago took its name from the condition of the surface of the country, which is hilly and rolling. The first white settler within the present city limits was Jeremiah Arnold, who erected a wood shanty for occupation during the winter of 1834-35. Adam Howder, whose name stands conspicious as the first permanent resident, was delegated by Hiram Greenman, of Utica, New York, Salem T. King and Alonson G. Budlong, land owners, to look after their interests; this was in 1835, and at about this time the original hamlet had its beginning. Previous to this time the country for miles around was little more than a wilderness, no other mark of civilization being apparent than the turnpike leading to Chicago, which was the only thoroughfare.

The original site of the city was located on the present fair grounds, but owing to chancery proceedings between Budlong and Greeman it made it impossible to give a perfect title to the land and the present location was substituted. In December, 1835, Greeman sold his interest to Rockwell Mauning and George C. Gibbs, the latter gentleman soon after selling his portion to Chauncey W. Ferris and John P. Cook who came early in 1836 and made Hillsdale their residence. Charles Gregory and William E. Boardman purchased interests here at this time and the owners of the property were known as the Hillsdale Company; this unincorporated company had for its principal object to make the young and thriving town so inviting as to be able to contest with Jonesville in competition for the county seat; Jonesville became the headquarters for the county in 1835, the records and business having been transacted previously at the seat of Lenawee county. Jonesville remained the county seat until 1843.

The first effort towards the establishment of the county seat at Hillsdale was made in 1839. It met with much opposition from the north part of the county; a counter-effort, as it were, was made by some Jonesville parties who succeeded in obtaining an act of the legislature by which the county seat was established at Osseo, March 31, 1840, with the provision that county buildings be erected there. No steps having been taken to comply with this requirement, the legislature passed an act in January, 1843, permanently locating the county seat at Hillsdale. A small building was immediately erected for the habitation of the county officials, where the present building stands. Later in the same year, there being no suitable building in which to hold court, an edifice was erected for the purpose of making it a house of worship, and also a place for holding the courts. The present court-house was erected in 1850-51 and has done good service for Hillsdale county these many years; its external and internal appearance being now far from modern, however the building has been the mark for much derogatory comment for some time past. An effort has been made to vote an appropriation several times, but the rural element has always voted down the question.

Soon after the arrival of John P. Cook and Chauncey W. Ferris, and during the same year, they built a saw-mill and a frame house; the water-power had its source in Baw Beese lake, which partly lies now within the city limits. (A sketch illustrative of Baw Beese lake appears elsewhere.)

In the spring of 1837 Joel McCollum came from New York state and together with Messrs. Manning, Cook and Ferris purchased lands lying north of the original plat, the present Bacon street of the city being the south line of the purchase; this puchased may be regarded as the initiatory step towards the laying out of the city.

Adam Howder, hale, hearty and hospitable, was the first landlord in Hillsdale. Finding his first log house incapacitated, a new structure 28x40 feet in dimensions was erected in '38. This building was two years later abandoned by Landlord Howder, who finding his old location too far away, erected a new tavern here in 1841 and christened it the Hillsdale House. (A more complete enumeration is made of hotels of the city in another place.)

The first flouring mill was erected here in 1838 by Messrs. Cook and Ferris; this plant absorbed most of the milling patronage of the county and was an important element in the business development of the locality. Other mills located in Hillsdale since then are F. W. Stock's City Mills, purchased of Cook & Ferris; Elliott's City Mills and Freed Bros'.

The Lake Shore (then known as the Michigan Southern) railroad was constructed and trains run through Hillsdale in 1853.

Henry Waldron, who was a civil engineer of ability, settled here in 1838 and was employed in the construction of the new road.

In ten years after the first settlement had been made Hillsdale had made a phenomenal stride and presented a remarkable example of prosperity.

In 1855 Messrs. Charles T. Mitchell, Henry Waldron and J. P. Cook embarked in a private banking enterprise with a capital of $17,000, opening on Broad street and continuing business until 1864, when Messrs. Mitchell and Waldron purchased the whole interest. It afterwards was merged into the Second National bank.

At this time (1864) the village became involved in litigation with Joel Joel McCollum, of Lockport, New York, who laid claim to that portion between Howell and Broad, now covered by the Waldron block, and brought suit to establish his claim arguing that the ground was private and not owned by the village. McCollum placed a building upon it and the village authorities tore it down; he then began suit in the United States courts, and the case is a memorable one from the interest it excited and the array of legal talent employed on both sides; by consent of both parties a judgment was obtained, and Henry Waldron purchased the disputed ground for $1,500 and erected upon it, the present Waldron block.

The first village election was held the 12th day of April, 1847. The following gentlemen were elected: President, Patrick McAdam; assessor, Chauncey Stimson; trustees, Harvey A. Anderson, Elijah Hatton, Henry L. Hewitt, Thomas Bolles and Isaac VanDenbergh.

The first city election was held in April, 1869, the city having obtained a charter at that time. Those elected were: Mayor, George W. Underwood; treasurer, Henry King; clerk, S. Chandler; aldermen, Samuel J. Lewis, Edwin J. March, Jas. G. Bunt, Benj. Fisher, Wm. Wilson, Wm. Pettis and Spencer O. Fisher.

One incident in the city's history since the early period, worthy of noting, was the artesian well project begun in 1872. A committee of three were appointed in

April, '72, to solicit subscriptions; an appropriation of $1,500 was made, and the location having been decided, it being on court house square, work was begun; funds having been expended another appropriation was made of $5,500; after boring to a depth of nearly 1,500 feet the undertaking was abandoned.

The first newspaper published in the county was the Hillsdale County Gazette; politically it was an adherent of the Jeffersonian Democratic school. The first number was issued at Jonesville, April 13, 1839. In May of 1843 it was removed to Hillsdale. The paper passed through several hands until 1855 when the office and appointments were purchased by N. B. Welper who removed it to Three Rivers and remained until 1859; he then returned to Hillsdale and established the paper again under the name of the Hillsdale Democrat, which title it bears at the present time. H. B. Andrews and Wm. H. Tallman purchased the sheet in 1866; Mr. Andrews retired from the firm in '67 and the paper was conducted by Mr. Tallman until 1886, he then disposing of his interest to E. A. Blackman. After Mr. Blackman's death in May, 1892, the management fell into the hands of the present editor, II. C. Blackman.

The Whig Standard was first issued June 30, 1846, by J. G. Clark and H. B. Rowlson. In 1850 Mr. Rowlson became sole editor and proprietor; its name was changed to the Hillsdale Standard, in 1855, the year of the organization of the Republican party. The paper is now owned and published by H. B. Rowlson & Son.

The Hillsdale Leader was first issued September 29, 1882, by Ackerly, Bowman & Co. The ownership of the paper finally fell into the hands of Col. E. J. March, who now together with Geo. K March conducts the sheet under the firm name of E. J. March & Co. Its politics have since the first number been Republican.

The Telephone-News was established in the summer of 1893 by A. H. English and W. H. Bowman. The paper is the result of the combination of the Reading Telephone, formerly conducted by Mr. English at that village, with the North Adams News, the property of Mr. Bowman. The paper is without political affiliations.

. The College Herald, a weekly college paper, the only college sheet in the world issued every week in the year, is published at the Commercial department of Hillsdale College by the College Herald Co. Alex. C. Rideout is the editor and publisher.

The Collegian, a bi-weekly sheet, is issued by students of Hillsdale College during the academic year. The paper was first issued during December of 1893. It will be published during the coming year by the faculty and students of Hillsdale College.

HILLSDALE COLLEGE.

Amid the December snows of 1844, in an old deserted store at Spring Arbor, Jackson county, Mich., with one teacher and with four boys and one girl as undergraduates, was opened the institution which has since become Hillsdale College. This institution owes its origin to the efforts of a few Christian men who deeply felt the the need of a school where young people could receive a Christian education. This led to the erection of two new buildings costing about a thousand dollars each, and to an increase in the teaching force. As there were at this time but few union schools and only one college in the state, it is not surprising that a large number of young people eagerly availed themselves of the educational advantages thus furnished. It soon became evident that more room would be needed. This forced upon the trustees the question as to where the institution should be permanently located. It was decided to remove from the site then occupied to some town which was situated on a railroad. Propositions were received from several places, but the one from Hillsdale was accepted by the faculty. The people of Spring Arbor were greatly incensed, and did all in their power to prevent the execution of this plan. Some threatened the teachers with violence, and concealed books and apparatus, while others served injunctions to prevent the removal of the college charter. Hence, but little more of the college was removed than its prestige, students and faculty.

Forty-one years ago the eminence of the village of Hillsdale, now known as "College Hill," was alternately crowned with waving grain and used a pastureground for the cattle of its owners. Here rose, in 1853, the walls of Hillsdale College, the corner-stone being laid July 4th of that year. The twenty-acres, which constituted the college grounds, were the gift of Esbon Blackmar. The proposition of the town to the college authorities included the gift of $15,000 for building purposes, *provided*, that an equal sum be put into endowment by the trustees. The proposition was accepted, on condition that said amount should be raised in the county, which was done, and the subscription of citizens were even increased to $35,000. The first college edifice consisted of five adjoining buildings, four of them 40x60 feet, and one 60x60 feet. They were so far completed that the school was opened November 7th, 1855, with four professors besides a principal of the ladies' department. These were Rev. Edmund B. Fairfield, A. M., president; Rev. Ransom Dunn, professor of Mental and Moral Philosophy and Natural Theology; Rev. C. H. Churchill, A. M., professor of Latin and Greek Languages; Rev. H. E. Whipple, A. M., professor of English Literature and History and Mrs. M. G. Ramsey, preceptress.

The objects sought by the founders of the college will be seen by the following extracts from the constitution and articles of association:

"The object of this institution is to furnish to all persons who wish, irrespective of nation, color or sex, a literary and scientific education as compehensive and thorough as is usually pursued in other colleges in this country and to combine with this such moral and social instruction as will best develop the mind and improve the hearts of the pupils.   *   *   *   A majority of the board of trustees, not less than two-thirds nor more than three-fourths, and a majority of the faculty, in which majority the president shall be included, shall always be members in good standing in the Free-Will Baptist denomination."

The school at the time of its opening at Hillsdale was composed of two departments—the academic and the preparatory. The first contained three courses of study, the classical, the English and the ladies', each of which included the studies which are usually found in a four years' course in American colleges. The last two were united in 1872 and called the scientific and ladies' course. The same year an academical course was arranged to meet the wants of those pupils who wished to complete some regular course of study, but who could not devote the full time required of candidates for degrees. A philosophical course was added in 1878 and the scientific course somewhat changed. Both of these omit the Greek and retain but little of the Latin, in order to give more prominence to the modern languages, mathematics and elective studies.

In 1876 an English and Normal course was established, which in 1878 was made a Normal course of two years, and which in 1884 was made a four years' course. In 1893 a special course in the Science and Art of Teaching was arranged for in accordance with the statute which provides that those who pursue any of the regular four years' and take this special course as an elective may receive the state teachers' certificate.

In 1884 F. B. Dickerson, of Detroit, having pledged five hundred dollars towards the erection of a gymnasium, the subscription for its construction and equipment was carried to about twenty-five hundred dollars, and a tasteful building 40x70 feet was dedicated in 1885, the first one in the state.

Since the opening of the institution a number of changes have been made in the board of instruction. The College has had six presidents, Rev. Edmund B. Fairfield, D. D., LL.D., elected 1855; Rev. James Calder, D. D., 1869; Rev. Daniel M. Graham, D. D., 1871; Rev. De Witt C. Durgin, D. D., 1874; Rev. R. Dunn, D. D., 1884; Geo. F. Mosher, LL.D., 1886 to present time.

The endowment since 1856 has been increased as follows: In June, 1862, the paid up endowment was $16,448.87; the invested fund in 1877, $93,295.45; in 1884, $137,802.69; in 1888, $159,987.65 and in 1894 it amounts to $217,395.23.

In the fall of 1862 the Free Will Baptist General Conference voted to appropriate $8,000 towards the endowment of a chair of theology to be known as the Burr professorship. In 1863 Rev. R. Dunn was transferred to this new department. Additions were made to this endowment till it now stands at $10,000.

Ever since 1855 instruction has been given in vocal and instrumental music; it was very irregular and varied in degree of excellence until 1863 when Fenton B. Rice took charge of the department. In the fall of 1869 Professor Melville W. Chase succeeded Professor Rice; subsequently Professor Chase was transferred to the Pianoforte, Harmony and Theory department and succeeded by Professor Graves in tone culture, who in turn was succeeded by Professor Dixon J. Churchill, who now has charge of the instruction given in Voice Culture.

The early history of the Art Department relates incidents of hard struggling before it could support a thoroughly competent teacher. In 1867 George B. Gardner took charge of the department and it is still under his supervision.

Early in the morning of March 6, 1874, three of the five college buildings burned, causing a loss of some $10,000 besides much valuable apparatus. Steps for rebuilding were immediately taken. The plan which was finally adopted for the new arrangement of the buildings embraces four disconnected buildings, which occupy the center of a park of twenty-five acres, adorned with well grown shade trees and evergreens. The buildings are of brick, three stories high beside the basements, and are arranged on three sides of a quadrangle with the principal front to the south. The building in the center is known as College hall; the west building, Knowlton hall; between Knowlton and College halls is Griffin hall; the east building, Fine Arts hall; between Fine Arts and College halls is the ladies' dormitory, which is what remained of the old building. The College library contains nearly nine thousand volumes.

The college societies that have been formed are: The Amphictyon and Alpha Kappa Phi organized in 1857; the Ladies'

GEO. F. MOSHER, PRES.

Literary Union and the Germanæ Sodales organized at the close of the same year. The Theadelphic was organized in 1867. All are still flourishing and form an important feature in the social life of the college. The college fraternities having chapters here are the Delta Tau Delta, established here in 1867, the Alpha Tau Omega in 1888 and the Phi Delta Theta somewhat earlier. The sororities are Kappa Kappa Gamma and Pi Beta Pi.

The last step forward taken by the College and worthy of especial note was the estabishment in the winter term of 1894, of a military department. Lieutenant E. A. Helmick, of the 4th Infantry, was detailed by the United States government to give instruction in military science and tactics and this detail was accepted by the College. This department has proved very popular and the beneficial effects of the military drill has been remarked by many observers. The cadet gray uniform has been adopted and the students already carry themselves with quite a soldierly bearing. Cadet army rifles and two rifled cannons have been ordered, and arrangements are being made for target practice the coming year.

Hillsdale College has always been progressive and aims to do honest, thorough work in the class room, and its influence is wholesome and far reaching.

THE COMMERCIAL DEPARTMENT.

The school known as the Commercial and Telegraphic department of Hillsdale College was opened in September, 1866. It occupied the third story of Union block, and was owned and managed by Calkins, Griffin & Co., Hon. Charles P. Griffin, now of Toledo, O., principal. The building was wrecked by falling soon after the opening, the school suffering loss of all its furniture, apparatus and supplies. Temporary quarters were occupied at the corner of Howell and McCollum streets, until Union block was rebuilt, the following year. In 1868 the school was transferred to Griffin, Drake & Co., and the same year was sold to A. C. Rideout, the present owner and principal. Early in 1870 the location was changed. Apartments were leased of Hillsdale college, and remodelled to suit the needs of the school, which became associated under a special contract with the college, nominally as a department, but having no organic or real connection.

When the college buildings were burned 1874 Professor Rideout, under agreement with the college authorities, erected Griffin hall for the special use of his school. It cost, with its equipment, about $20,000, and is the best

A. C. RIDEOUT.

building on the campus. No commercial school in the northwest, perhaps in the whole country, is provided with more commodious and convenient apartments, and better facilities for carrying on the work of commercial education than are here afforded. The building is of modern design, 72x52, four stories, brick and stone. The two upper stories are divided into twenty-seven dormitories. The lower stories are used for lecture and practice purposes. Throughout, the structure is admirably adapted to the uses for which it was designed. Every practical facility is provided for giving instruction in all the branches of commercial education. The commercial course, perpetual scholarship $30, books and blanks $10, embraces practical book-keeping, penmanship, business arithmetic, political economy and commercial law. All the work is practical. The graduate from this course is competent to keep accounts in any branch of business. In the actual business department the drill is most painstaking and thorough. Over forty sets of stock and partnership books are opened, the transactions recorded in all their details, analyses made, settlements effected and the ledgers closed. Students receive constant personal attention, and all work is closely criticised and corrected. The most thorough drill is required in all forms of commercial paper, and business correspondence. Stenography and type-writing are also taught, but for these branches extra tuition is charged. A practical course in telegraphy is a prominent feature of the institution, perpetual scholarship $35, books $3. The best modern apparatus is provided, and students are drilled in all the details of operating until well prepared for office work. Instruction is also given in all branches of electrical science. Hundreds of practical book-keepers and telegraph operators have gone out from this school. Students are never drilled in classes. The work is entirely personal from the beginning to the close. No piece of work is ever allowed to be the result of joint efforts. Each must master the work for himself, and become independent in the application and practice of principles. Much stress is put upon practical execution. It is a school where the student learns to *do*, as well as to think and plan. The plan or scheme that he cannot execute in practice he learns to regard with disfavor.

In the management of this school Professor A. C. Rideout has always been alone and independent. He has provided wholly for its support, and has been financially responsible for all of its affairs. Its business has always been transacted in his name and upon his credit. He has always prescribed the studies, employed his assistants and directed the work for the school. Into this work he has put twenty-eight years of his life and more than $25,000. Aside from his own school, he has accomplished much in other lines, having been identified as a successful worker in many community enterprises, the details of which cannot be given in this limited sketch, but are well known by the local public. His age is fifty years. He was born in Ohio, and was educated at Brilliant and Oberlin. The last year of the late war he served as a private in the 110th O. V. I. in the Valley of the Shenandoah. In 1876 he received the honorary degree LLD. from Muskingum College.

GRIFFIN HALL.

HILLSDALE PUBLIC SCHOOLS.

The history of the schools of Hillsdale seems to begin back in the early 30's. A school house was first erected within what is now the city limits in 1835. It was located on Bacon street east, on the site now occupied by G. L. Segner's residence. Another building was constructed for school purposes at the same time that the court house was built, and like the present "palace of justice," its walls were of stone. This building was torn down (it occupied the present jail site) in 1868. The present central building was erected in 1868. It is a model three-story high school structure. Within its walls have been educated many of Hillsdale's professional and business men besides many others who have departed for other fields of labor and study.

The school consists of twelve grades, each grade requiring one year of work. Those holding diplomas from the English, Scientific or Latin courses are admitted to the courses corresponding in the University of Michigan at Ann Arbor without further examination. The average attendance of the high school is about 130.

W. L. SHUART, SUPT.

The number in the graduating class this year, '94, was 19.

There are four ward buildings, instruction being given at these buildings up to the 8th grade. The pupil is then transferred to the central building to complete the other four grades.

The total enrollment of pupils in the public schools during the year 1893-94 was 896. The total number of those of school age in the city last year was 1,182.

The officers and instructors for the ensuing year are:

MEMBERS OF THE BOARD.—S. C. Rowlson, F. H. Stone, C. F. Cook, C. S. French and C. W. Terwilliger.

OFFICERS OF THE BOARD.—Moderator, S. C. Rowlson; Director, F. H. Stone; Assessor, Chauncey F. Cook.

COMMITTEES.—Finance—French, Terwilliger, Rowlson; Repairs—Terwilliger, Cook, Stone; Supplies—Rowlson, Cook, Terwilliger; Text-books—Cook, Stone, French; Teachers—Stone, French, Terwilliger; Library—Cook, Rowlson, Stone.

TEACHERS—Central building, Samuel J. Gier, Principal; Emma DuBois, Preceptress; Lottie Tyler, 8th grade; Rena Ayars, 7th grade; Agnes M. Woods, 6th grade; Aimee Baker, 5th grade; Cora Martin, 3d and 4th grades; Frankie Atwater, 1st and 2d grades; H. A. Castle, janitor in-chief. First Ward school, Millie Troy, 7th and 8th grades; Gevevieve Lyon, 3d and 4th grades; Millie A. Corning, 1st and 2d grades; Irving Dean, janitor. Second Ward school, F. Lenora Gaskins, 5th and 6th grades; Caroline Dudley, 1st and 2nd grades; N. W. Harrington, janitor. Third Ward school, Nora McBain, 3d and 4th grades; Susie Kinnie, 1st and 2nd grades; H. B. Granger, janitor. Fourth Ward school, Mary Robertson, 1st and 2nd grades; Miss Robertson, janitor. Special Teachers, Lelia I. Smith, Instructor in Music; Nellie E. Montgomery, Instructor in Latin; Rev. F. K. Bauer, Instructor in German, Civil Government and Astronomy.

THE HILLSDALE FAIR.

The Hillsdale County Agricultural Society was organized in February, 1851, at a meeting of farmers held in what was then Underwood's hall, where the Woltmann block now stands, in Hillsdale village, in response to a call made through the public press. A constitution and by-laws were drawn up, presented and adopted at this meeting. The officers elected at this first meeting were: Hon. Henry Packard, of Jonesville, president; three vice presidents; Hon. J. P. Cook, treasurer; Isaiah H. McCollum, corresponding secretary; Henry II. Ferris, recording secretary and an executive committee of one from each township in the county. The first fair was held in October, 1851, on the court house square in Hillsdale village, the square being used as a show ground and the "temple of justice" itself being taken for an exhibition hall. The show was not very extensive either out or in doors; the number of entries in all departments was less than a hundred, and the sum of the premiums less than eight dollars. This amount and the expenses were raised by subscriptions, no admittance fee being charged.

In the fall of 1852 the second fair was held on the public square in Jonesville, around which a high board fence was constructed, and to which an admission fee was charged of half a dollar for annual family tickets and ten cents for single ones. Both the number of entries and the amount of receipts were nearly double those of the previous year. In 1853 for the first time the society had what might be considered as its own grounds; about an acre of space was secured on the corner of Vine and Union streets (Hewitt's grove). This was surrounded by a factory cloth fence, wherein was held the third annual fair.

The next year, 1854, land was leased of Jonathan B. Graham at Jonesville and fitted up for fair purposes. This year a catalogue was published, a short track was prepared for exercising horses and posters sent throughout the country. The result was a spirited county competition in cattle and horses, and the addition of swine, sheep, poultry and a few mechanical and agricultural implements to the list of exhibits. There were nearly 500 entries and $400 taken for dues and admissions. In 1855, the officers procured the use of a part of the land now occupied by the association. In 1857 the exhibition was held at Jonesville; the entries numbered 903 and the receipts $700.

Down to 1859 the society had no permanent grounds; in that year a committee was appointed to take steps regarding a permanent location. On their report the board decided to locate the grounds within a mile fo the court house. Accordingly, a contract was made with Cook & Ferris to purchase seventeen acres constituting a part of the present grounds; seven acres on the south end for $50 per acre and ten on the north for $100 per acre. All subsequent fairs have been held on this ground. There was some ill feeling in the north part of the county regarding the permanent location at Hillsdale and the fair for 1860 was not as successful as some of its predecessors. On this account, too, the Farmers', Mechanics' and Stock Breeders' Association was organized, which held meetings annually in Jonesville and only existed a few years. At the end of that time the stockholders sold their land for railroad purposes and since then the Hillsdale County Agricultural Society has received the warm support of all who are interested in institutions of this nature. During the war years, 1861-64, the attendance and exhibits were small, but in '65 after the peace proclamation, the soldiers being back, generally with plenty of money, the fair was a success, the receipts reaching the enormous sum of $1,550 and placing the society out of debt except for its land. In 1865 $2,000 was expended in fencing and otherwise improving the grounds. In 1866 the receipts swelled to $3,300, which went in part payment on notes amounting to $2,500 that had been given out a short time previous.

In 1878 the society was entirely free from debt and after paying every indebtedness had $302 left in the treasury.

The Hillsdale Fair is no longer a "county fair." It is the largest fair held in the state at the present time, its total number of paid admissions being more in one day (Thursday) than the state fair was during the entire week of the same year. This was the red letter day in the history of the fair, there being on that occasion 35,000 people being upon the grounds at one time. The accompanying scene gives a fair representation of the crowd on that day.

The society now has 60 acres of land all fenced in and equipped with the best of buildings requisite for purposes of a fair. There are seven halls, a mammoth tent, three-quarters of a mile of sheds, two barns, a grand stand and one of the best judge's stands ever built. The first racing course was constructed in 1858 and was a half-mile "kite shaped track," it being the first track of that description ever constructed; this was merely accidental, however, as the lay of the grounds compelled them to build a track kite shaped. Little did the fathers imagine they were laying out the first, to be afterwards famous, kite shaped racing course.

Another feature of these grounds is the perfectly shaded grove of native oaks, maple and evergreens and other ornamental trees.

The entries of late years have averaged 4,000 annually and the receipts between $11,000 and $12,000. The largest day of the fair was Thursday in 1892, there then being 35,000 people on the grounds. The large days of other years have been close to 30,000 admissions.

The success of the fair in late years is due in great part to the hustling and energetic secretary, John F. Fitzsimmons; under his management the fair has gained an almost national popularity and a credit and financial condition such that the society has not had to ask for a guarantor in order to induce exhibitors to make displays and compete for premiums.

BAWBEESE LAKE.

Baw Beese Lake together with four other lakes and their surrounding parks form a picnic and excursion resort of no small reputation. Away back in the early days it took its name from a Pottowatomie Indian chief who was a "big injun" about here in the 30's and early 40's. About 1870 was the first that this now celebrated place became a popular excursion ground.

Its reputation extended far and wide; this happy chain of circumstances existed until the year 1876; on August 1st of that year occurred a drowning accident which completely put a stop for a time to any further excursions and picnics to Baw Beese Park. Although the lake or park management of that time were entirely blameless and faultless as regards this event, yet the superstitious and even those who never admitted such weakness, gave Baw Beese a wide berth. Of late years however, this drowning incident has begun to assume a less vivid aspect and now picnics are again being held there. Consequently the pristine popularity is once more returning. In 1891 the Lake Shore & Michigan Southern Railway company purchased Baw Beese park. Through the efforts of this company large excursions have been and are now being run to this point. The grounds have been improved, summer resort parapheranalia, such as bathing houses, water toboggan slide, row boats, dancing pavilion and other appointments, go to make up a very convenient summer resort for picnic and excursion parties. The Lake Shore company have announced that a large and commodious hotel building will be established at this park and be ready for the 1895 business. If this be the case the only lacking necessity will have been supplied and Baw Beese will be one of the swell summer resorts of Michigan, for which this glorious commonwealth has a national repution.

The park is this season under the personal management of N. J. Widger, a successful manager, whom the Lake Shore people were fortunate to secure to superintend the grounds and take charge of the management in general. Through Mr. Widger's efforts every excursion or picnic that has held forth at Baw Beese this summer has received most courteous treatment and the best of everything the place can afford.

CHURCHES.

A. T. SALLEY.

This church was organized Nov. 24, 1855, Hillsdale College being under the control of the Free Will Baptist denomination. The membership is and always has been, largely made up of the faculty, students, friends and supporters of that institution. At first services were held in the College chapel, but in 1867 the large edifice was constructed at the corner of Fayette and Manning streets at a cost of $30,000. For the first sixteen years the preaching was done by members of the faculty, Rev. E. B. Fairfield, H. E. Whipple, R. Dunn and J. Calder having served as pastors. Rev. R. Woodworth, of Greenville, R. I., was chosn pastor Sept. 30, 1871, remaining two years. Rev. A. A. Smith began his pastorate May, 1874, and served till January 1, 1878; Rev. DeWitt C. Durgin, D. D., from 1878 to 1883; Rev. Ashum T. Salley and C. D. Dudley were associate pastors until 1884; at that time Professor Dudley removed, since which time Rev. Salley has very ably and acceptably filled the pastorate of this church.

METHODIST CHURCH.

P. J. MAVEETY.

The organization of the Methodist church in Hillsdale dates back to 1842. The first regular services began in that year, being held in a school house with Rev. Thomas Jackson as pastor-in-charge and Rev. G. H. Shurtliff as assistant. In 1845 during the pastorate of Rev. Wm. Pitt Judd a plain, but commodious house of worship was erected. This building was destroyed by fire in 1863, in the second year of Rev. Thomas Comfort's ministry; the present edifice was built two years later in 1865; Rev. Thomas Lyon was then pastor. The church is now in a prosperous condition, being practically free from debt and growing steadily in its membership. The number of names now on its rolls is 400. The Sabbath school has an equally large membership, with an average attendance of nearly 300. It has a library of 400 volumes.

The pastors that have served and date of pastorates are: Rev. Thomas Jackson, 1842-44; Adam Minis, 1844-45; Wm. Pitt Judd, 1845 47; Wm. Kelly 1847-48; Henry Worthington, 1848 50; Rev. Buchanan, 1850 51; Alex. Campbell, 1851 53; F. W. May, 1853-54; Ira B. Card, 1854-55; D. D. Gillett, 1855 56; Joseph Jennings, 1856-57; Jeremiah Boynton, 1857-59; L. D. Earl, 1859 61; Thomas Comfort, 1861 63; Thomas Lyon, 1863-65; Mr. Dunton, 1865-66; Noah Fassett, 1866-68; Geo. Lee, 1868 69; H. H. Parker, 1869 70; Wm. Daust, 1870-72; George Hickey, 1872-73; Thomas Jacobs, 1873-74; Ira R. Wightman, 1874-77; Augustus F. Gillett, 1877-78; Andrew Fitch, 1878-79; Levi Tarr, 1879 81; A. R. Morrison, 1881 83; J. G. Crozier, 1883-85; M. D. Carrell, 1885-87; G. C. Draper, 1887-90; A. E. Craig, 1890-93. P. J. Maveety is the present pastor.

PRESBYTERIAN CHURCH.

J. A. CRAWFORD.

A meeting for the organization of a Presbyterian church was held in the village school, July 22, 1843, presided over by Rev. William Page, of Jonesville. At this meeting "Articles of Faith and Covenant" were adopted and a deacon and three elders were elected; William Cross and Allen Hammond were elected elders, one for two years the latter for one year; Thomas Bolles was chosen deacon. The church started out with fourteen members, the first Sunday service being held in the village school house, July 23, 1843. The school room was occupied for some months, when a building used for court purposes was used as a worshipping place. The present edifice was erected in 1853. The church was received into the Presbytery of Marshall at Albion, January 30, 1844. It subsequently joined the Presbytery of Monroe, with which it is now connected.

The pastors in their order since the organization of the church are: Rev. Elijah Buck, 1843-45; Thomas P. Emerson, 1845-46; Philip Titcomb, 1846-47; William Page, 1847-48. Rev. William S. Taylor, the first regularly installed pastor, 1850 to May, 1853; Calvin Clark, February 1854 to July 1858; James Knox, October, 1858, to October, 1861; Frederick Gallagher, 1861-69; Volney A. Lewis, December, 1869 to December, 1872; Samuel B. Bell, January, 1873 to 1875; Leroy V. Lockwood, February, 1876 to 1879; Charles N. Waldron, 1879 to 1882; James M. Barkley, 1882-85; Rev. Mr. Millham, 1885-87; Rev. Mr. Sexton, 1887-91. John A. Crawford came in 1891 and has been pastor since.

E. M. GRIFFIN.

The Baptists of Hillsdale organized a church on November 11, 1848. The young church flourished for four years; then followed a season of discouragement and decline which culminated in the granting of letters of dismission to the members January, 1855. For nearly fourteen years thereafter the Baptist church was practically dead. Some of the members joined neighboring churches. Subsequently a branch of the North Adams church was organized at Hillsdale, which became an independent church the next year.

The present church was organized October 1, 1869; the church was organized by an ecclesiastical council February 2, 1870; A. B. Prentice and A. G. Stewart were ordained deacons. The pastors have been thus far: Rev. H. Gallup, 1870-71; then followed a period of relapse until April 1, 1875, when A. E. Stone was ordained as pastor and remained as such until April, 1878; A. J. Furman, October, 1878-80; B. E. Hutchinson, January, 1881 to June, 1884; E. F. Osborn, July, 1885 to September, 1886; J. C. Rooney, May, 1887, to September, '88; Rev. H. Burns, October, '89 to '93. Rev. E. M. Griffin who became pastor in '93, still presides over the congregation.

ST. ANTHONY'S ROMAN CATHOLIC CHURCH.

FR. P. J. SLANE.

This parish was established in 1853. Rev. Father Kendricken, a native of Belgium, who first settled at Monroe came as frequently as his pastoral duties would permit, which was seldom oftener than once in two or three months, and said mass at private houses in the village. A society of this denomination was finally organized; an edifice of the Presbyterian society was purchased and converted into a Catholic church. Rev. Charles Rychart took charge of the parish and was resident pastor fourteen years; Rev. Father Dreesen succeeded him and remained two years; after a short interval Rev. Father Duhig came, staying five years. His successor was the present pastor, Rev. Father Slane. Since Father Slane's advent, a new church edifice has been erected as well as a commodious parochial residence.

GERMAN LUTHERAN CHURCH.

REV. F. C. BAUER.

The German Evangelical Lutheran Trinity congregation of Hillsdale, Michigan, was founded in the year 1849 by Rev. W. Hattstaedt, of Monroe, Michigan, and organized in 1854 by Rev. Ph. Trautmann, of Adrian, Michigan, who supplied the congregation until 1860. The church which is still used as a house of worship was built in 1854. Rev. H. Speckhardt, Sr., was the first pastor residing in Hillsdale. He was called in 1860 and stayed till 1863. The following ministers have served the congregation: Rev. W. Hattstaedt, 1849-54; Rev. Ph. Trautmann, 1854-60; Rev. H. Speckhardt, Sr., 1860-63; Rev. J. Hahn, 1863-73; Rev. J. A. Schroeppel, 1874; Rev. G. Schieferdecker, 1875-77; Rev. M. Toewe, 1878; Rev. Halboth, 1880; Rev. H. Speckhardt, Jr., 1882-85; Rev. F. Dryer, 1886-88; Rev. F. C. Bauer, the present pastor, entered his duties in October, 1888, being called from Greenville, Michigan. The congregation has seen many a trying day and was on the verge of ruin, caused mainly by too frequent changes of pastors. It is doing quite well at present showing a steady gain of membership. The present membership is about 200. There is a ladies' society with thirty-eight members, a young people's society called "*Der Jugendbund*" with forty-four members and a choir of eight members. All the societies are under the supervision of the pastor. The parochial school, Rev. Bauer, teacher, averages fifteen pupils. The property consists of church, school-house and parsonage (free from debt) and is located on Griswold and South srreets, east. The services are conducted in the German language.

ST. PETERS' PROTESTANT EPISCOPAL.

The Protestant Episcopal church in Hillsdale in the early days was under the fostering care of the mother church at Jonesville. Rev. Darius Barker, rector of Grace church, Jonesville, held the first service in the village of Hillsdale, in the hotel of Adam Howder, one Sunday in November, 1839. The reverend gentleman often visited the place for the purpose of holding services after that. Further missionary work was done by successive rectors from Jonesville during the following twenty years. Removals of church families from Jonesville to Hillsdale increased the number of workers so that a mission was established in Hillsdale, September 10, 1844, under the title of St. Peter's church. In March, 1858, a re-organization of the church was effected under the revised statute of 1857. The present church building was erected in the summer of 1858.

The first resident rector was Rev. Gilbert B. Hayden, of New York, who served in 1859-60. Others in their order are: Gerret E. Peters, 1860-67; John W. Buckmaster, 1868-69; Henry H. DeGarmo, 1869 70; Wm. W. Raymond, 1870-79; William J. Lemon, 1879-83; Theodore L. Allen, 1883-86; F. W. Bayley-Jones, 1886-89; Robert C. Wall, 1891 93; the rectorship at present, is vacant.

SEVENTH DAY ADVENTISTS.

The rise of this denomination is comparatively of recent origin, dating back not to exceed thirty-five years. Believers in the new advent of Christ have existed since about 1834, when under the preaching of William Miller from that time till 1844, many thousands in the country embraced his views and fully believed the advent of the Lord would take place in 1844. Without stopping to discuss the correctness or incorrectness of his position or in any way explaining the causes of the disappointment that overtook the believers, we will simply say that from that time till now there has existed a people known as Adventists.

Soon after 1844 a few persons who had previously expected the advent of Christ in their study of the Scriptures became fully convinced that it was their sacred duty to keep holy the seventh day of the week instead of the first, and immediately began its observance and to teach others their views. This was done by preaching and publishing. In the course of ten or twelve years 'the number of seventh day observers had so increased that they numbered thousands, but as yet had taken no denominational name.

In October, 1860, at a conference of leading men in Battle Creek, Michigan, who observed the seventh day, they voted to adopt the name of "Seventh Day Adventist" as a denominational name. They also legally organized a conference, publishing association and other organizations for the transaction of business.

The Seventh Day Adventist church of Hillsdale, Michigan, was legally organized in Novembr, 1860, by Elder J. H. Waggoner, and articles of association adopted and trustees elected. They also elected a local elder and two deacons. The first meeting house was erected in 1857 by the company of believers who had previously embraced the Advent doctrines under the labors of Elders Waggoner and Cornell. This house stood on Oak street on a corner of the premises owned by A. F. Fowler. Services were held every Sabbath (Saturday) at 10:30 and Wednesday evening prayer meeting. The number of charter members who first signed the covenant was thirty-seven. The congregation continued to worship in the house first erected until 1886, when the growth and needs of the congregation demanded a larger structure, and they purchased a lot on the corner of Oak and Vine streets and built a more commodious and substantial frame building with a seating capacity of about 250.

The membership of the church numbers about seventy, most of whom reside in and around the city. There is a Sabbath school with a membership of about fifty, also a missionary society having for its object the dissemination of denominational literature, and charitable and benevolent purposes.

There are no settled pastors with a fixed salary permanently or temporarily hired by any organized church of Seventh Day Adventists, but all the ministers of the denomination are evangelical in their labors, carrying the gospel into new fields and establishing new churches, and are supported from a fund created by the tithing system, so that the church of Hillsdale has no settled pastor. However, it frequently enjoys the labors of ministerial brethren who often visit them, as well as the labors of Elder D. H. Lamson, an ordained minister of the conference who permanently resides in the city.

This people being a prophetic people raised up to do a special work of giving the last message of warning to the world before the coming of Christ, are necessarily aggressive in their work, and are so organized that nearly every one takes an active part in extending the work.

The church doors are always open to welcome all who may feel disposed to come in and worship.

CENTRAL COLLEGE BUILDING.

FREE WILL BAPTIST CHURCH.

FIRST BAPTIST CHURCH.

METHODIST EPISCOPAL CHURCH.

PRESBYTERIAN CHURCH.

ST. PETER'S EPISCOPAL CHURCH.

L. S. & M. S. R'Y YARDS.

THIRD WARD SCHOOL BUILDING.

A CLASSIC RUIN—HILLSDALE COUNTY'S COURT HOUSE.

CENTRAL HIGH SCHOOL BUILDING.

SCENE AT THE HILLSDALE FAIR.

SCENE AT THE HILLSDALE FAIR.

A VIEW OF BAW BEESE PARK.

CITY DIRECTORY,

1894.

ADDITIONS AND CORRECTIONS.

This list comprises names and addresses of all those having taken up residence in the city since August 1st. And also those that have been omitted from the regular list. The regular list, or Directory proper, commences immediately after these Corrections and Additions, on Page 32.

Abbreviations used are: S, school, student, or south; dom, domestic; n, north; e, east; w, west; r r emp; railroad employe.

B.

Barger, Chas, laborer, 1 Howell.

Boag's City Bakery, Fresh bread and cakes; ice cream parlors and lunch room, 68 Howell st, n.

C.

Cole, L. F., dealer in groceries, choice, fancy and staple, game dressed, poultry and farm produce, 52 Broad n.; res 96 Hillsdale.

Cory Adelbert, dealer in high grade pianos and organs; band and orchestra music furnished for all occasions; Broad street opposite Keefer house.

Corson, Levi H, grocer, bds. Keefer house.

Croose, W. H. & Co., dealers in fresh and salt meats, oysters and canned goods, vegetables in season, 96 Broad s.; res 58 Oak.

Corson, **Levi H.,** staple and fancy groceries, No. 70 Howell n.; fresh fruits and berries a specialty in their season; goods promptly delivered in any part of the city; terms cash; prices right; res Keefer house.

For anything to be found in a First Class Drug Store go to CHAS. S. FRENCH'S.

32   HILLSDALE CITY DIRECTORY.

D.

Delavan, E. C., Veterinary surgeon; attends all calls promptly; 27 years experience in the profession; res and office 53 Broad n.

Depot Dining Hall, S. C. Rowlson, proprietor; Mrs. E. M. Eggleston, manager; first class in every particular.

F.

Fabey Ann, 36 Manning s, domestic.

Fast Delmer, attorney-at law; office over Goodrich's drug store.

Fredonia Washer Co., manufacturers of Fredonia Washers; J. S. Parker, manager; Art O. K. Parker, secretary; agents wanted everywhere; office 21 Broad n.

Fumman Robert, Hallet st, farmer.

G.

Gardner Geo. F., dealer in general hardware, plumbing, steam heating, furnace work, hose, belting, fittings for steam and water and bicycles; 20 Howell; res 46 Manning n.

Green E. W., city retailer of illuminating oils and gasoline; res 221 Hillsdale.

Gillett Anna, 1 Howell s.
" Hannah, "

Gillett Daniel, 1 Howell s.
" Tony E, "

L.

Lyon Frank A., attorney at law; room 27 Waldron block; res 60 Manning s.

M.

Martin Geo F, 17 St. Joseph, barber.
" Sarah J, "

Meyers Verne E, 32 College e.

Maveety Susan E, 41 Manning n.

P.

Peterson A. T., proprietor of city livery and feed stables, 38 McCollum, opposite engine house; res corner McCollum and Manning.

Ranney E. L., dealer in groceries, provisions and feed, 41 Broad n; res 102 Howell n.

S.

Stewart John E, 1 Howell s.

T.

Taylor Mark W, 83 West n, harnessmakr.

W,

Wagner Belle S, 62 Waldron.

Watts Nora, 1 Howell, domestic.

Whitney Dilworth L, 1 Howell dining-room girl.

(The Directory Commences on Opposite Page.)

All

Abbott Harriett, 71 Budlong.
" Ira, 71 Budlong, carpenter.
Adams Charles W, 1 Howell, carpenter.
" Edgar E, 101 Oak, farmer.
" Elizebeth 73 West S.
" James R, 89 Norwood ave, laborer.
Adams Kate, 89 Norwood av.
" Lena, 268 West N, s.
" Mary E, 101 Oak.
" Strickland, 73 West S, retired farmer.
Agnew Allen, 15 Bacon W, retired farmer.
" R. Ann, 15 Bacon W.
" Hugh, 15 Bacon W. s
" Ruey 15 Bacon W, teacher.
Albaugh Charles, 68 West N. jeweler. (See Albaugh & Son.)
Albaugh Ernest R, 68 West N, jeweler. (See Albaugh & Son.
Albaugh Lizzie, 59 Broad S, domestic.
" Margarett, 68 West N.
Albaugh & Son, Chas L and Ernest R: jewelers and opticians; a fine stock of watches, jewelry and silverware, 68 Howell.
Alger Herbert O, 40 College E, traveling salesman.
Alger Lida, 40 College E.
Allen Anna Bell, 51 Railroad W, domestic.
" Ella, 51 Railroad W.
" George, Howell S, laborer.
" Geo W, 51 Railroad W, laborer.
" Lavilla E, Howell.
" Lyda, 108 Hillsdale W, s
" Maud May, 51 Railroad W, domestic.
" Theodore, " " " laborer.
" William B, Howell.
" Wm. S, Howell, traveling salesman.
Alles Elizabeth, 73 Broad S, dressmaker.
" Elizabeth, 73 Broad S.
" Henry, 73 Broad S, carriage manufacturer.
Alles Maggie, 73 Broad S.
" Minnie, 73 Broad S, dressmaker.
" Lillie, 73 Broad S. s
Allis Dilla May, 16 W College. s
" Eliza A, 16 W College.
" Wm J, 16 W College, bookkeeper.
Alexander Fannie, Baw Beese Park.
" Lucius F, " laborer.
Alley Bert S, 31 State, machine agt.
" Chas, 29 Vine, machine agt.

Ay

Alley, Cora, 11 Norwood av W.
" Emma E, 29 Vine.
" Estella, 70 Howder.
" Flora M, 31 State.
" Fred C, 11 Norwood av W, barber.
" Lee, 70 Howder, painter.
" Walter J, 29 Vine, laborer.
" Lella M, 29 Vine, drug clerk.
Alvord Chas H, 74 Manning S. s
" Luella M, 74 Manning S.
" Melinda, 74 Manning S.
Ammerman Celestia, 227 Manning N.
" DeWitt, 227 Manning N, carpenter.
Anderson Elizabeth, 147 Manning N.
" Eunice M, 112 College E.
" Harriette A, 244 Union N.
" Kate, 147 Manning N, dressmaker.
" Luella L, 244 Union N. s
" Margaret, 147 Manning N, dm.
" Seth V, 244 Union N, carpenter.
Andrew Ella S, 11 Oak, works in tannery.
" Lucy R, 11 Oak.
Andrews Emeline, 226 Bacon E.
" Francis J, 226 Bacon E, farmer.
Andrus Gertrude M, 201 Union N.
" Justin A, 201 Union, in tannery.
Armstrong Adelaide, 37 Howell S.
Armstrong Carrie, 12 Manning N, serv.
" Caroline, 37 Howell S.
Ashbaugh Carrie L, 208 West N. s
" Elvira A, 208 West N.
Atwater Adeline, 91 Broad S.
Atwater Frances J, 91 Broad S, teacher.
Armstrong Geo, 70 Howell S, shoe maker.
Ashbaugh John B, 208 West, salesman.
Armstrong John W, 23 Broad S, retired merchant.
Ashbaugh Lewis E. 208 West N. s
Armstrong Marietta L, 23 Broad S.
" Martha, 70 Howell S.
Arnold Mary C, 46 Broad S.
" Wilson B, 46 Broad S, miller.
Alsbro John T, 37 North, hardware clerk.
" Sarah H, 37 North.
Austin Darius S, 229 Union N, gardener.
" Lewis B, 229 Union N. s
" Mary E, 229 Union N.
Avery Mary J, 56 Broad S.
Ayers Anna, 31 State, dressmaker.
" Claude C, 31 State.
" Geo W, 31 State, carpenter.
" Mary E, " "
" Ray E, " "

Ba

Ayars Renet, 47 Broad, teacher.
Bach Carrie, 186 Bacon E.
" Carrie R, Bacon E.
" Catherine, 35 Short.
" Henry, 186 Bacon E, plumber.
Bachman Anna, 93 West S.
" Bertha H, 87 West S.
" John C Jr, 87 West S, cutter.
" John C, 93 West S, clothing mcht.
Bachmayer Maggie.
Baer Edward C, 78 Budlong, architect.
" Barbara A, 78 Budlong.
Bail Alex P, 1 Howell S, restaurant.
" Chas A, 3 Lake, cigar maker.
" Ellen J, 1 Howell S, cook.
" Ester, 42 St Joseph, laundry.
" Lucinda, 16 Ferris.
" Mary H, 3 Lake.
" Nancy, 16 Ferris.
" Wm A 16 Ferris, weaver.
Bailey Carl L, 82 Oak, stenographer.
" Cora D, 82 Oak S.   s
" Frank, 245 Hillsdale, teacher.
" Harry G, 82 Oak, lawyer.
" Henry, 102 Budlong, barber.
" Lyrena, 102 Budlong.
" Minerva, 245 Hillsdale.
" Sarah S, 82 Oak.
Baird Frank, 1 Garden, laborer.
" Maggie, 1 Garden.
" Melon, 1 Garden, cigar maker.
Baker Cora B, Railroad W.
" Edward, 114 Howell S, salesman.
" Ella B, 34 Garden.
" Elma, 68 West S.
" Frank E, 34 Garden, contractor.
" Fred L, 78 State.   s
" Harper V D 78 State, mail carrier.
" Henry, 13 Howell S, machine agt.
" Jane, 284 West N.
" Jennie, 15 West N, servant.
" Julia W, 284 West N.
" Julius, 36 Budlong, grocery clerk.
" Lewis S, 68 West S, salesman.
" Mariah L, 78 State.
" Mary, 36 Budlong, dressmaker.
" Sarah D, Railroad W.
" Wm E, Railroad W, painter.
" Wm T, 176 Manning N, brakeman.
Baldwin Angie G, 104 Hillsdale.
" Ella, 104 Hillsdale, teacher.
" Ella, 102 Howell S, domestic.
" Frank, 104 Hillsdale, R R clerk.

Be

Baldwin Wm, 104 Hillsdale, salesman.
Bangs Flora, 202 Manning N.   s
Barkley, Samantha, 103 Budlong.
Barker Aimee, 4 Manning S, teacher.
" John, 34 Short, laborer.
" Martha, 34 Short.
Barnard Cora M, 15 Mechanic.
" Geo E, 15 Mechanic, minister.
Barnes Ernest, 81 Broad s.   s
" Amos, 69 West S, painter.
" Catherine, 2 Howell N, cook.
" Christina, 35 Champaign.
" Ernest, 1 Howell, laborer.
" Geo W, 35 Champaign, engineer.
" Ira G, 27   "   blacksmith.
" Ira W, 35   "   clerk.
" Minerva, 27   "
" Sarah E, 81 Broad S.
" Susan, 69 West S.
Barnhart Frank, Broad N, laborer.
" Henry, 55 Oak, farmer.
" Lucinda, 55 Oak.
Barnlocker Barbria, 13 Cemetery.
Barnum Electa, 217 Railroad E.
Barre Carrie A, 54 Manning N.
" Corvis M, 54 Manning N, lawyer.
Barrows Evander W, 47 Howell S grocer.
" Martha, 47 Howell S.
Bartholomew Eliza A, 42 McClellan.
" D H,   "   laborer.
Bartlett Minnie, 41 West N.
" Nicholas,   "   R R clerk.
Bassell Bart R, 40 Spring, tailor.
" Teassa G, 40 Spring.
Batchelder Kingford, 225 Union, c Prof.
" Mary A, 225 Union N.
Bates Cyrus, Spring, laborer.
" Hattie, 9 McCollum.
Bath Emma G, 46 Manning s.
" Oliver C, 46 Manning s.
Bauer Elizabeth, 211 South e.
Bauer Ferdinand C, 211 South e.
Pastor of the German Lutheran church;
instructor in German in city public
schools.
Bauer Johanna, 211 South e.
Baxter Ida M, 381 Hillsdale.
" Jas H, 381 Hillsdale, farmer.
Beam Louise M, 240 West n, teacher.
Beath Anna, 29 Manning s.
Beck Catherine, 262 Bacon e.
" Clara J,   "   "   domestic.
" Emma,   "   "   tailoress.

Kochenthal Bros. & Co., Leading Clothiers, Furnishers & Hatters.

Bi

Beck, Geo F, 9 North, laborer.
" Minnie, between Bacon and South.
" Samuel, laborer,   "   "   "
Beckhardt Edward, 90 Howell s, grocer.
" Geo, 1 Howell, clerk.
" Louis, 60 Howell s, grocer.
" Martha J, 90 Howell s.
Beggars Mabel G, 91 West n.
Belcher Myrtle, 237 Hillsdale, laborer.
Belding Edd, 122 Broad n, laborer.
Bell Chas O, 98 West n, pension agt.
" Edgar F, 27 Reading av, painter.
" Elias B, 98 West n, pension agt.
" Emeline, 27 Reading av.
" Ethel L, lives in college building.
" Jane, 98 West n.
Bellamy Mary Ann, 6 Sharp e.
" Shephard S,   "   farmer.
Belman Edward, 22 Manning n, coach'n.
Bemus Albert, Bernard, laborer.
Benjamin Cora C, 228 Manning n.
" Ruben, 228 Manning n.   s
Bennett Margaret, 200 West n.
" Timothy,   "   laborer.
Bently Anna L, 82 Howder.
" Allen, 80 Hillsdale, upholster.
" Clara I, 74 Howder.
" Geo W, 74 Howder, farmer.
" Isabelle, 216 Manning n.   s
" Lena B, 80 Hillsdale.
" Mary H, 74 Howder.
" Wilbur, 82 Howder, farmer.
Bentz Edward T, 6 St Joseph, mill eng.
" Jennie,   "
Berg Della, 104 Broad s, compositor.
Betts Archibald, 93 Railroad w, salesman.
" Kate, State, teacher.
" Ella, 251 West n.
" Julia A, State.
" Stephen,   "   farmer.
" Susan, 93 Railroad West.
Bidwell Irene, 20 Sharp w.
Bigelow Mark, 75 Bacon e.
Bigler Maud, 69 Howell s.
Bildner Mary, 13 Cemetery.
" William,   "   miller.
Bird Ada, 28 West n.
" Amelia E, 249 Union n.
" Day, 212 Manning n.   s
" Francis E, 249 Union n, farmer.
Birdsley John, Dutch hill, cooper.
Bishop Lavina, 67 St Joseph.
Bishopp Margarett, 38 West n.

Bo

Bishop Addison G., violin-maker, gun
and locksmith and all other kinds of
fine work in repairing; can repair
musical instruments; have been in
Hillsdale for 27 years. All work done
at reasonable prices and on short notice.
Hillsdale street.
Bishopp Spencer D, attorney and so-
licitor in chancery. Room 18 Wal-
dron block. Collections a specialty.
Black mar Cornelia, 107 State.
" Minnie J,   "   teacher.
Blackmer Chas, 32 Railroad, electrician.
Blackman Daisy C, 113 Hillsdale, teacher.
Blackman Hiram C, 113 Hillsdale.
Editor and proprietor of the HILLS-
DALE DEMOCRAT.
Blackman Louise M, 133 Hillsdale.
" Pearl C, 113 Hillsdale, compositor.
Blakeman Ray, 14 Manning n, merchant.
" Mary   "
Blood Adeline, 1 Cemetery.
" Henry,   "   carpenter.
Boag Archibald, 18 Bacon w, baker.
" Christina,   "   clerk.
" David   "   baker.
" John   "   "
" Mary   "   "
Bodine Morell J, 66 St Joseph, laborer.
Bolls Amiziah, 65 State, carpenter.
Bolles Amaziah H, 30 Howell, bill poster.
Boue Frank W, 16 Howell n, tel opr.
" Kate C,   "   hair dresser.
Boone Frank, 131 Bacon e, carpenter.
" Serena,   "
Bonney Florette, 81 College e.   s
Bosenbark Dora, 84 College e.
" Tena,   "
Botsford Nathan, 74 Broad s, laborer.
Bottrell Margaret, 23 West n, domestic.
" Sarah   228   "   "
Boutwell Celia J, 54 Manning n.
" Mabel,   "
Boutwell Wm. B., Photographer,
Waldron block; fine crayon work a
specialty; artistic portraits guaranteed.
Bowditch Charlotte, 97 Sharp e.
" Mabel, 206 Manning n.   s
Bowen Clara, 29 Short, stenographer.
Bowman Fannie A, 108 Broad s.
" Wm H, 108 Broad s, publisher.
Boycott Mary, Bernard.
" William,   "   butcher.

See Boyle & Brown, the Corner Dry Goods Store.

French's Soda Fountain Dispenses Comforting,
Cooling, Drinks to the Tired and Thirsty. Try them.

36   HILLSDALE CITY DIRECTORY.

Br

Boyington L D, 37 Mechanic, minister.
" Marilla, "
Boylan Nathan J, 6 Sharp w, carpenter.
Boyle & Brown, L R Boyle, O N
Brown; dealers in dry goods and
cloaks and notions; 46 Howell.
Brackett Sadie, 224 W n.   s
Bradley Anna W, 207 Union n.
" Chas "
" Geo S, " minister.
Bradshaw Wm W, 185 Broad s.
" Nettie, "
Branch Gertrude, 198 Hillsdale n.   s
" Minnie, 108 Howell s.
" Walter R, "
Brearly Edward, 262 West n, salesman.
" Ellen H, "
" Maud, " s
Brecht Agnes, 8 Monroe.
" Erl, " r r employe.
Breed Clara, 215 Hillsdale.
" Clara Bell " s
" Ida, " dressmaker.
" Jonathan " teacher.
Bricker James I, 211 Manning n.   s
" Joana, . "
Briggs Adelaide, 16 Railroad.
" Clarrisso, 80 Howell.
" Darius, 11 Norwood av n, teamster.
" Edgar, 20 West s, laborer.
" Frank L, 16 Railroad, laborer.
" Geo, 96 Howder, painter.
" Jennie, 20 West s.
" John N, 11 Norwood av n.
" Lillie E, 96 Howder.
" Warren, 80 Howell, painter.
Brightman Frances, 206 Manning n.
" Francis, " machinist.
Brooks Arthur U, 98 Sharp e, barber.
" Clara, 98 Sharp e.
Browkaw Joe, 55 Broad s.
Brown Abbie L, 28 w.
" Amy, 140 River e, domestic.
" Celestia, 107 Union.
" Chas A, " clerk.
" Clyde, 28 Ferris, laborer.
" Daniel L, 182 Hillsdale, merchant.
" Ellen E, 28 West n.
" Emily, 77 Broad s.
" Etta, 88 Fayette e, tannery.
" Grace, 126 Hillsdale.
" Ida E, 28 Howell s.
" Immanuel, 28 West n, farmer.

Ca

Brown, May L, 94 West s.
" Nellie, 182 Hillsdale.
" Oliver N, 28 Howell s, merchant.
" Wm, 94 West s, blacksmith.
" Wilson E, 126 Hillsdale.
Bruble Lula, 71 Oak, domestic.
Brush Anna, 38 Manning n.
" James, 107 Howder, laborer.
" Libbie, "
" Millie, 10 Howell s, tailoress.
Bryan I T, 11 West n, jeweler.
" Jennie, 32 Manning n.
" Joseph, Bacon w, laborer.
" Maggie, "
Bryant E G, 268 West n.   s
" Mary L, 12 Waldron.
Buchanan Louise, 59 Manning n.
" Louise S, "
" Wm T, "
Buckingham Harriette, 98 West n.
Budd Clinton L, jeweler, watch maker
and repairer; repairing of all kinds
done on short notice and at reasonable
rates; Woltmann block, res, 48 Howell.
Budd Marian, 48 Howell s.
Bulles Nancy, 28 Ferris.
Bump Alfred, 127, Fayette w, laborer.
" Lillie, "
Bunting Mary, 173 Manning n.
Burdick Mauerc C, 158 Hillsdale.
" Wm H, " teacher.
Burgdolph Addie, 12 Ferris.
" George " blacksmith.
Burgdolt Anna W, 20 Budlong.
" Fred, " clerk.
Burges Mary E, 10 West s.
Burnan Moses S, 52 Union, minister.
Burns Ester, 32 Garden.
" Geo F, 95 Manning s, cooper.
" Mary, "
Burton Hannah, 25 St Joseph.
" Henry, " farmer.
" Robert, " cigar maker.
Burwick Mary, 16 West n.
Butler Edward, 185 Manning s, porter.
Butler Burt, 185 Manning s, clerk.
" Frances, "
" Jane, "
" Mary, "
" Norman " broom maker
Button Gail 2 Howell n, bell boy.
Cadwell C A, 3 Howell s, cigar maker.
Callaghan John, 84 Spring brakeman.

Ca

Callaghan Julia, 84 Spring.
" Thos, " tinner.
" Dennis, " cigar maker.
" Patrick, " laborer.
" Michael, 163 " r r employee.
" Mary " "
Calder Bert, 82 Norwood av, brakeman.
" Jennie E, "
Camp Emery, 148 Howder, laborer.
" Sarah J, "
" C Daniel, 223 Bacon e, laborer.
" Anna M, "
Campbell Albion, 23 Reading av, lumber.
" Jane, "
" Harry, " clerk.
" Kate, " s
" Edwin C, 83 Howell s, lumber.
" Cornelia, "
" Benj, 187 Bacon e, teamster.
" Margaret, "
" Louise, 96 Howder.
Canfield Henry, 44 Fayette, laborer.
Cap Tressa, 28 Howell s, domestic.
Carey Katie A, 15 Railroad.
" Dow H, " conductor.
Card Ira B, 103 Howell s, clergyman.
Carr, Carrie V, 290 West n.
" Albert E, " minister.
Carpenter Ira, proprietor horse shoeing shop 41 Bacon e, opp Smith's livery stables, res 107 Howell.
Carpenter F A, 240 West n, teacher.
" Lydia.
" Chas C, 16 Bacon w, blacksmith.
" Hattie May, "
" Jas S, 207 Griswold, cigar maker.
" Nettie, " "
" Susan, "
Carpenter Irene, dealer in fine millinery. 10 Howell s, res same.
Carter Chas H, 39 Howell s, farmer.
" Mary R, "
" Lizzie, 23 Marion, dressmaker.
" Geo E, Wolcott, farmer.
" Maggie M, "
Cass Chas, 177 Manning n. s
Castle Frank A, 103 West s, carpenter.
" Harriett M, "
" Hiram A, 24 West s, school janitor.
" Elizabeth, "
" Thos, 89 German, laborer.
" Minnie. "
Catherman Clarence, 230 Manning n. s

Ch

Chadwick Wm C, attorney at law; office rooms 90 Howell 2d floor front suite; res 51 Broad.
" Geneva, "
Chambers Wm, 252 West n. s
" Maggie, 91 " domestic.
Chamberlain S G, 2 Howell, train disp.
Chandler Harriett, 21 Budlong w.
" John A, 21 Bacon w, mechanic.
" Marion, "
" Harriett H, 174 Hillsdale.
Chapin Benjamin, 31 Bacad n, baggage.
" Jennie, 66 State.
Chapman Clarence H, 63 Barry, mcht.
" Mary M, "
" Wade W, " "
" Nora, 38 Broad s, milliner.
" Mary, 2 Howell n, cook.
Chappell John J, 52 Union, farmer.
Chase Melvin W, 157 Hillsdale, mc prof.
" Eleanor, "
" Minerva, 273 Hillsdale.
" Mary E, "
" Paul W, 225 Hillsdale. s
Chatfield, 9 Lake, postal clerk.
Chestnut Jas T., attorney at law; circuit court commissioner and solicitor in chancery. Office r 1 Underwood bk, res 84 South w.
Chestnut Andy, 86 South e, dep sheriff.
" Frances, " teacher.
" Ada, "
" Mary, 29 South w.
" Wade, 62 Howell, carpenter.
Chester Guy M., attorney at law prosecuting attorney for Hillsdale county, rooms 16 and 17 Waldron block, res. 46 Broad s.
Chester Martha, 46 Broad s.
Childs Wm B, 67 Broad s.
Chillson Henry, 173 Hillsdale, teacher.
Chilson Chas A, 80 Fayette e, accountant.
" Mary A, " teacher.
" Mattie B, " violinist.
" Fadelia, "
Chittenden Myrna, 94 Broad, laborer.
Choate Anna, 15 Railroad w.
Churchill Dixon J, professor of voice culture choral director in Hillsdale college; room 28, art building; residence 80 College e.
Churchill Frances M, 80 College e.
" Lucia N, "

FRENCH'S PRESCRIPTION DEPARTMENT is in
Charge of Careful and Experienced Druggists.

38   HILLSDALE CITY DIRECTORY.

Co

Clapp Nathan F, 95, Broad s trainer.
" Mariah, "
Clap Cora, 46 Broad s.
Clark Jas M, 242 Bacon e, fruit grower.
" Mary E, "
" Francis P, "
" Elihu S, 81 College e, piano tuner.
" Mary A, "
" Frank J, 81 West n, laborer.
" Sarah, "
" Silas T, 238 Park, stone mason.
" Mrs S T, "
" Harry, 183 Hillsdale. s
" Marial, 15 Ferris.
Crittenden Elmer, 17 Railroad, ph'rm'c'st.
" Nella A, "
Crume John T, 44 Howell s, dentist.
" Alice N, "
Crum Eugene H, 216 Manning n, clerk.
" Malisa H, "
" Nelly T, "
Clement Charlie, 3 Howell, laborer.
Clifford Wm, 79 Spring, r r employe.
" Mary, 79 Spring.
Clickner Oliver, 122 Railroad n, cond.
Clossen Ana, 182 Hillsdale. s
Cochran Maggie, 50 Salem.
Colman Fred, 108 Oak, tannery.
" Jennie E, "
Cole Lincoln, 96 Hillsdale, grocer.
" Fannie, "
" Andrew J, 95 College e, harness m.
" Mary, "
" Sidney, " s
" John, 122 Railroad n, carpenter.
Collins Clate, 219 Manning n, s
" Newton, 87 Manning s, farmer.
" Anna, "
" Cora, 2 Howell n. waiter
Columbus Lurch, 18 Logan, huckster.
" Tibbie, 18 Logan.
Comer Sarah, 38 West n, servant.
Comstock Sam A, 216 West n, farmer.
" Catherina, "
Common Chas, 121 Fayette e, tannery.
" Susan, "
Coomba Lotta C, 208 West n. s
" Emily A, "
Coon Joel, 114 Oak, carpenter.
" Jennie E, "
" John, 64 West s, laborer.
" Frank, 122 Railroad n, barber.
Conklin George, 58 Manning s, cooper.

Co

Conklin Mary, 58 Manning s
" Frank, 92 Howder, cooper.
" Lizzie, "
" Frank H, 97 Howell s, private sec.
Copeland John D, 110 Railroad w, car.
" Fannie, "
" Joseph, 183 Hillsdale. s
Conolly Robert, 14 Railroad w, laborer.
" Anna, "
Corson, Henry, 94 Broad, screen factory.
Condra Cora, 89 Norwood av, seamstress.
Converse Russel, 75 Bacon e, sheriff.
" Carrie D, "
Cook Wm, 52 Howell, bk agt.
" Silvia W, "
" Chauncey, 27 Broad s, banker.
" Louise "
" Martha, 139 Hillsdale.
" Kate "
" Jennie, 74 Broad s, boarding house.
Cooper Wm, 79 Budlong, machine agt.
" Effie "
" Samuel, 13 St Joseph, brick mason.
" John " fireman.
" Sarah "
Copp John S, 213 Union n, professor.
" Ellen A, 213 Union n, teacher.
" Mabel " s
Corning Lucy A, 42 Union.
" Mildred A, " teacher.
" Anna B, " compositor.
Cory Hiram H, 86 Sharp e, laborer.
" Fanny R, "
Corey Linus F, 173 Hillsdale, train disp.
" Lusetta M, 198 Union n.
" Agnes F, 173 Hillsdale.
" Adelbert, 198 Union n, musician.
" Elizabeth " stenographer.
" Amos, 21 Champaign, jeweler.
" Margarett "
" Stella, 38 Howell s, domestic.
Cornell Joseph, 23 Marion, laborer.
" Ida C "
" Orvie J, West s, law student.
Corlett Robert, 8 Railroad w, carpenter.
" Amelia "
Corwin Wm O, 72 Broad s, machinist.
" Josephine "
" Jane A "
Coryell Mateland, 30 St Joseph, dec'ratr.
" Mary "
" Hannah, 14 "
Costly Wm S, 252 West n. s

Cu

Cottrell Eliza, 40 Howell s.
" Lydia "
" R Dwelly " machine agt.
" Elsie " dep reg deeds.
Coughlin Jane, 2 Howell n, laundress.
Cousins Lewis, 93 Mead, meat market.
" Frank " "
" Cris R " tannery.
" Chas " laborer.
" Sarah A "
Cowan Christopher, 84 Marion, laborer.
" Mable "
Cozzens Fred, 30 Short, butcher.
" Jenny "
Crago Ellen, 42 River.
" Archie " s
" Sula "
Cramner John, 89 Barry, electrician.
" Carrie "
Crane Stephen, 44 Budlong, bk.
" Lucy "
" Hannah, 4 Manning s.
Caruthers Elizabeth, 44 Railroad e.
" Oliver " farmer.
Crater Ellen L, 14 Railroad.
" Mary 114 Hillsdale.
Crawford Rev. J. A. pastor of the Hillsdale Presbyterian church.
Crawford Blanche T
Crippen Richard A, 14 Manning s, clerk.
" Ann "
Crisp Geo C, 84 Sharp e, farmer.
" Joseph " "
" Louisa "
Crocker Horace, 97 Railroad w, teamster
" Della W "
Crofoot Eva M, 252 West n. s
Croose Robert J, 12 Howell s, butcher.
" Adeline, 12 Howell s.
" Nellie " dressmaker.
" Wm, 58 Oak, butcher.
" Mary A "
" Joseph, Spring, farmer.
" Theresa "
Crosby Unity J, 231 Manning n.
Crowell Olva L, Bacon e.
" Morris M " carpenter.
Croxton Hiram, Howell s, farmer.
" Martha "
Crozier Priscilla B, 324 Manning n.
Culver Clayton, 33 West s.
" Samantha "
" Edgar D " drayman.

Da

Culver, Mollie, 33 West s, milliner.
Cummins Jas, 121 Fayette e, salesman.
" Hattie "
" Lucy M, 225 Hillsdale.
" Cora E, "
Cunningham Edward H, dealer in coal, wood, ice, salt, lime, hair, brick sewer pipe, tile, cement and jobber in shelled corn. Office 32 Hillsdale; res. 138 Hillsdale.
Cunningham Ada C, 138 Hillsdale.
" Mable E, " s
Curtis Ransom, 104 Broad s.
" Leon, 97 Sharp e, horseman.
" Susie "
Cutler Fred J, 100 Union, clerk.
" Mary E "
Daggett Georgie A, 140 Oak.
" Peter O " tannery.
" Wm, 63 Marion, farmer.
Dalley Cora A, 15 Railroad w.
" Wm S " laborer.
Dancer Edna, 198 Hillsdale n. s.
Daniels George B, 67 Marion, tel op.
" Lucius A " laborer.
Dargett Mary, 50 Spring.
" Wesley " r r employe.
Daugherty Frances, 65 Budlong.
" Mitchell A " laborer.
Davenport Alice, 231 Manning n.
" Edith L " dressmaker.
" John " horse trainer.
Davies Chas, 6 Railroad. s
Davis Ada, 294 West n, music teacher.
" Alberta W, 208 Hillsdale n.
" Almond G, 89 College e, r r emp.
" Andrew J, 292 Hillsdale n, minister.
" Armageon, 89 College e.
" Chas A, 142 River e, tannery.
" " W, 127 Fayette w, laborer.
" Ellen E, 292 Hillsdale n.
" Elmira, 294 West n.
" Flossie E, 206 " p o clerk.
" Geo R " druggist.
" Hulda L, 142 River e.
" John, 42 River, drayman.
" John E, 78 Reading av, laborer.
" Laurens P, 292 Hillsdale n, clerk.
" Lucretia, 127 Fayette w.
" Mary J, 208 Hillsdale n.
" Maxwell H, 89 College e, r r emp.
" Myrtle S " clerk.
" Myrtie M, 206 West n, elocutionist.

Di

Davis Pheosen, 19 Vine.
" Sarah, 62 Howell, domestic.
" Sophia S, 296 West n.
Day Casius, 114 Broad n, clerk.
" Mattie, "
Dean Alexander, 98 Bacon w, wag. makr.
" Edna A, 11 State. s
" Irving W " merchant.
" John D " clerk.
" Rachael R "
" Lavina, 30 Griswold.
Decker Annie, 11 Waldron.
" Herbert " milkman.
" Elsie, 44 Fayette w.
Deery Charlie, 99 Spring, cigar maker.
" James " peddler.
" Margaret "
" Theresa "
Delaney Joseph, 59 Hillsdale, laborer.
" Julia "
" Wm O " laborer.
Delevan Ed C, 53 Broad n, vet surgeon.
Delmire Fred, 249 South e, farmer.
" Maggie "
Democrat, Weekly Newspaper; one of the oldest papers in Southern Michigan; fine job work; excellent advertising medium; rates reasonable.
Denison Delia, 13 Howell s.
" Ida, 72 North, domestic.
Denney John, 68 North, painter.
Denning Alice M, 183 Hillsdale, domestic.
Denver Bridgett, Spring.
" James " laborer.
Depew Azariah, 86 Howell s, carpenter.
" Nancy M "
Dewey Alice, 224 West n. s
" Almira "
" Nathaniel, 99 Howell s.
Dibble Bertha, 15 Manning n, blk k.
" May "
" Eda Bell, 35 Manning n.
" Edwin A " produce dealer.
" Fannie, 56 Manning s, dress maker.
" Juliette. "
" Timothy E, 56 Manning s, attorney.
Dickerson Lorenzo, 55 Broad s, salesman.
" Mattie J, 55 Broad s.
Dickinson Alva B, 2 Howell n, prop of Smith's Hotel.
Dickinson Fannie A, 2 Howell n.
" Mirah, 54 Ferris.
" Mary, "

Du

Dickinson Samuel, 54 Ferris farmer.
Defiler Bennie, 46 Howell s, clerk.
" Henrietta, " dressmaker.
" Etta C " teacher.
" John A " carpenter.
" Willie E " painter.
Dilley James, 177 Bacon e, blacksmith.
" Marian W "
Dillon, Anna, 23 Ludlam.
" Frank " harness maker.
" Chas, 19 Short, laborer.
" Mary " washwoman.
" Thos " butcher.
Dingman Elmira, 211 Manning n, bk agt.
Disley Lotta, 50 Bacon w.
" Wm A " barber.
Dodson Chas W, 2 Howell n, hotel clerk.
Doragby Wm W, 59 Howell s, undertk.
" Hannah "
Doney Eva, 4 West s.
" Margaret "
" Minnie "
Donovan Jessie B, 21 State, milliner.
" Mary A "
" Michael J " carpenter.
" Vinnie E " teacher.
Dorr A W, 191 Hillsdale. s
Double Cynthia, 58 Salem.
" David L, " carpenter.
" Elmira A, "
Doud Nettie C, 183 Hillsdale, s.
" Mary E, "
Douglass Archibald, 6 Budlong, carp.
" Carrie M, 83 State.
" D J, 183 Hillsdale, s.
" Ellen, 6 Budlong.
" Grant, 183 Hillsdale, s.
" Harriett, 6 Budlong.
" John H, 83 State, r r brakeman.
Dove Alonzo S, 310 West, n. s
Dow Jennie M, 257 Union.
Driggs Anna, 11 Railroad.
" Lizzie, " domestic.
Du Bois Emma G, 47 Broad s, teacher.
" Humphrey, 47 Broad s, trav sals.
Dudley Caroline, 70 Fayette e, teacher.
Dulivan Ulick, 237 Hillsdale.
Dunnigan Albert P, 378 Manning n, eng.
" Belle C, "
" Jessie S, "
Dunn Rev. Ransom, De Wolf prof. of Homiletics in Hillsdale college, 192 Hillsdale n.

The Oldest

Wine is the finest in quality. It has had the time to become rich with the years.

The Quickest

Journal to publish the news, in this active age, is the most sought after, provided the happenings are chronicled in a crisp and concise manner, avoiding superfluity.

The Neatest

Printing, and that which aims at a happy combination of careful execution and low price, is the work that people like.

The Democrat

Is such a newspaper as that described above, and has a job printing equipment capable of turning out anything from a milk ticket to a book like the Hillsdale City Directory. Call and see.

Em

Dunn Serena, 192 Hillsdale n.
Dush Alice May, 50 Sharp w.
" Frank, " retir. farm.
" Melissa A, "
" Stephen, " s.
Dutcher Charles, 21 Manning n, hostler.
Dwight Jennie D, 297 Hillsdale.
Dwight Sylvester F., attorney-at-law and solicitor in chancery, a general law business; perfecting titles to real estate a specialty. Office over postoffice, room 18.
Dyer Samuel B, 297 Hillsdale, cab mkr.
Easling Bert G, Montgomery, laborer.
" Edward, " cem sexton.
" Sarah H, "
Easterly Barbara, 34 Cemetery, domestic.
" Edith, 14 West s.
" Elizabeth, 34 Cemetery.
" Emma, " domestic.
" Maggie, " tailoress
" Mary, "
" William, 14 West s, flour packer.
Ebersole Amos A, 202 Manning n, s.
Eccles Charles W, 20 Howell s, undertkr.
Eddy Walter, 11 Broad n, sexton.
Edwards Harriett, 68 West n.
" Harriette, 40 Welch.
" James, Spring, laborer.
" Stella, 68 West n.
Eggleston Cora, State, teacher.
" Ellen M, 42 Monroe, man. r r din, hall.
Eggleston Emaline, 148 Hillsdale.
Elco Eva, 50 St. Joseph.
" John, " laborer.
Ellington Al, 104 Broad n, blacksmith.
" Minnie, 184 Broad n.
Elliott Anna B, 152 Hillsdale.
" Bertha M, 185 Manning n, saleslady
" Erastus, " r r contr.
" Fay W, 152 Hillsdale n, miller.
" Kate E, 185 Manning n.
Ellis Francis G, 42 West n.
" Joseph, " shoe merch.
" Mrs Wm, 57 Oak.
" Wm, " clerk shoe store.
Ellsworth D. C, 76 College e, farmer.
" Hattie E, 41 North.
" Mary, 59 Manning n, domestic.
" Sarah, 76 College e.
" Smith, 41 North, painter.
Emerson Charles, 118 Hillsdale, servant.

Fa

Emmert Rosa, 280 Bacon e.
" William, " laborer.
Engelhardt Fred, propr. of the Keefer house barber shop; hair-cutting, shaving and shampooing; special attention paid to ladies' and children's work; bath room in connection; open week days; res. 41 Griswold.
English Amos H, 64 Barry, publisher.
" George, 12 Ferris, work in res.
" Ida, " "
" Lula, 64 Barry, compositor.
" Lydia, 83 South e.
" Martha E, 64 Barry.
Edsal Coe, 70 North, works in flour mill.
" Ida, 70 North.
Estey Edgar J, 20 Sharp w, carpenter.
" Ruth, "
Estell Jennie, Fayette w.
" Wm H, " laborer.
" Barton, 88 Hillsdale, cooper.
Evans Emma, 15 Ferris.
" Frank, " bookkeeper.
Evarts Walter, Budlong, trav salesman.
Everett Janette, 13 Broad s.
" Joseph, 110 Hillsdale, ret farmer.
" Lydia S, "
" Robert A, 13 Broad s, physician.
Ewing Cora A, 251 West n.
" Thomas E, " farmer.
Fahey Bridgett, 32 Garden.
" Martin, " drayman.
Fairbanks Bertha, 97 Budlong.
" Charles, 234 Bacon e, carp.
" Edgar, 97 Budlong, carpenter.
" Harrison, 234 Bacon e.
" Jennie, 97 Budlong.
" Minerva, 234 Bacon e.
Falconer Frank M, 219 Manning n.
Falley Adelia S, State,
Fant Anna, 101 Howder.
" John M, " grocery clerk.
" Martin, " "
" Mary, "
Fant T. M., 62 Howell n, dealer in Fancy Groceries and Table Luxuries; res. 101 Howder.
Farrand Etha, 14 Howell s, merchant.
Farley Eugenia, 219 Manning n, s.
" Eunice, " s.
Farnham Ann S, 80 McCollum.
" Edward, 1 Howell, fireman.

For Pure Drugs & Medicines Chas. S. French's.
⌒⌒×CALL AT×⌒⌒

48   HILLSDALE CITY DIRECTORY.

Fl

Farnham H. L., agent, 50 Howell; buy
  U. S. Express money orders; safest
  and best; receipt always given; Hills-
  dale, Mich; res. 80 McCollum.
Fellows Emma, 3 Railroad.
  " George, 87 State, teamster.
  " Jane J.
  " Samuel H, 3 Railroad, r r employe.
Ferguson Anna M, 44 Bacon w.
  " Maud E,   "   domestic.
  " Stephen,   "   cooper.
Ferris Charlotte, 94 Howell s.
  " Fred, 42 St. Joseph, work laundry.
  " Orren W, 94 Howell s, furn. deal.
  " Phœbe E, 9 North.
Ferris & Singer, 4 and 6 Howell s,
  dealers in furniture, carpets, etc; un-
  dertaking a specialty; piano moving
  done on short notice.
Fields Hiram, 89 Howell s, fruit grower.
  " Hiram Mrs,
  " Jennie,
Figel Wm, 15 Railroad w, r r employe.
Fillo Edwin, 102 Broad n, landlord.
  " Effie, 42 St. Joseph, work in laund.
  " Ellen, 102 Broad n, landlady.
Filson Earl, 12 McClellan, work sc. fac.
  " Margaret,   "
Finney Nancy, 3 Howell s.
  " Thomas,   "   r r conductor.
Fireman Arthur, 75 Bacon e.
First National Bank of Hillsdale,
  Mich., organized 1863; oldest National
  bank in Southern Michigan; capital
  and surplus $120,000; transacts a gen-
  eral banking business and pays interest
  on savings deposits. F. M. Stewart,
  president; C. F. Stewart, cashier; F.
  W. Prentice, assistant cashier.
Fish Edwin, 142 Hillsdale, ret. merch.
  " Louisa,   "
Fisher Belle, 38 St. Joseph.
  " Edna R, 4 Manning s.
  " Emily R,   "
  " Lotis A, 38 St. Joseph, clerk.
  " Sarah, 15 Manning n.
  " William R, 38 St. Joseph, mus.
  dealer.
Fite E. D. 191 Hillsdale,   s.
Flemming Adda C, 48 Welch.
  " Albert, 94 Oak, carpenter.
  " Clarence, 62 Bacon w, lineman
  " D. E, 48 Welch, carpenter.

Fr

Flemming Julia, 62 Bacon w.
  " Louie, 94 Oak, work in tannery.
  " Susan, 94 Oak.
Flint Francis, 67 Manning n.
Flint Jas R,   "   butcher.
Fogle Elsie, 71 State.
  " William,   "   laborer.
Folger Electa, 13 West s.
  " Hosea,   "   retired farmer.
Folsom Wortem H, 230 Manning n, s.
Foote Elizabeth, 85 Howell s.
  " Ford W,   "   hotel clerk.
  " George W,   "   mail car.
  " Wallace,   "
Force Ida, 4 McCollum.
Ford Augustus, 39 State, farmer.
  " Caroline, 85 Union, teacher.
  " Emily M, 8 Bacon e.
  " Henry M, 107 Mead.
  " Julia M, 93 Norwood ave.
  " Lydia E, 39 State.
  " Marquiso D. 93 Norwood, r r emp.
  " Sarah S, 107 Mead.
Forquer Fannie, 90 Norwood ave.
  " Sidney,   "   printer.
Fort Elizabeth, 37 St. Joseph.
Foskit Myron, 230 South e, laborer.
Foughty Stella, 12 McClellan, domestic.
Fowler Agnes L, 7 State.
  " Travis A,   "   carpenter.
  " Ida A, 99 Howder.
  " James W,   "   r r employe.
  " Pherdina, 7 State.
Fox Cynthia E, 163 Manning n. .
  " Fred B,   "   s.
  " Mary,   "
  " Mary,   "
Fancher Dillron, 12 Sharp w, carpenter.
Frankinfield H. H, 76 Howell s, barber.
  " Mary,   "
Frankenstein, Ed M, Howell s. (see
  Hillsdale Cigar Co.
  " Essie, 43 Waldron.
  " Isaac,   "
  " J,   "   clothing merchant
  " Minnie,   "
  " Minnie, Howell s.
Frankhauser Belle, 4 Manning s.
  " Isaiah E,   "   att'y.
  " Dorothea, 22 Bacon w.
  " Mary A,   "
  " Silas B,   "   M. D.
  " William H,   "   att'y.

Ga

Frankhauser Bros.; W. H. and E. I.; attorneys-at-law; room 23 Waldron blk.
Frantz Mary, 88 Fayette,
"   Philip,   "   harness maker.
Freed Ellen, 80 Spring.
"   Emma C, 73 Spring.
"   Henry H, 80 Spring, miller.
"   James, 73 Spring, miller.
Freland Alice, 214 Bacon e.
"   Henry,   "   flour packer.
French Caddie M, 84 Budlong.
"   Catherine G, 8 West n.
French Charles S, druggist and pharmacist; a complete stock of drugs always in stock; prescriptions carefully prepared; No. 8 Howell n; res. 8 West n.
French Ezekiel, 230 West n, grain buyer.
"   James H, 10 South w, drayman.
"   Joseph, 74 South e, retired farmer.
"   Laura M, 10 South w.
"   Louisa M, 74 South e.
"   Mary J, 10 South w.
"   Mattie, 230 West n.
"   Walter,   "   s.
French W. H., commissioner of schools for Hillsdale county; office room No. 25 Waldron block; res. 84 Budlong.
Frensdorf L. H., hatter and gents' furnishers 36 Howell n; res. 2 Bacon e.
Frensdorf Minnie, 2 Bacon e.
"   Regina,   "
Frisbie Blanche M, 41 Salem.
"   Charlotte, 11 Reading ave.
"   John L,   "   groc.
"   John L, 41 Salem, turner.
"   Minnie, 234 Manning n,   s.
Fuller Abigail S, Howell s.
"   Adelbert, 111 Mead, laborer.
"   Aleanzar, 82 Budlong, ret. farmer.
"   Amanda, 82 Budlong.
"   Eli A, Howell s, farmer.
"   Gertie,   "
"   Harvey A, 16 Mechanic, lecturer.
"   Jessie, 111 Mead,
"   Lottie, 216 Manning n.
"   Mayme, 216 Manning n,   s.
"   Reuben, Howell s, farmer.
"   Sadie W, 16 Mechanic.
Fulton Ethel, 225 Hillsdale, s.
Gaige Beulah, 45 West n, cashier.
"   Catherine   "
"   Frank   "   merchant.
"   Nellie   "

Gi

Gaige Orson H, 45 West n,   clerk.
Gaines Adelie, 11 West n.
"   Chas A   "   hotel clerk.
"   Permelia, 201 Hillsdale.
"   Willard   "   farmer.
Gale Dora, 29 Ferris.
"   Elizabeth   "
"   Horace H, 2 Howell n, restaurant.
Galliger John J, 74 Broad s, laborer.
Galagher Margaret, 73 Union.
"   Mary H   "
Galloway Edgar O, 10 Broad s.   law s.
"   James S   "   attorney.
"   Lizzie   "
"   Ava   "
Gardner Anna M, 80 McClellan.
"   Edmund   "   screen fac.
"   Ernest, 18 Garden, tannery.
"   E V, 191 Hillsdale.   s
"   Geo B, 64 McClellan, art prof.
"   Geo W, 46 Manning n, merchant.
"   Henrietta, 64 McClellan.
"   Gertie, 18 Garden.
"   Jennie C, 46 Manning n.
Garner Helen, 122 Broad n, domestic.
Garrett Jennie L, 3 West n.
"   Lulie B   "
"   Nathan M   "   salesman.
Garrison Curtis S, 187 Union n, ret mcht.
"   Elizabeth   "
"   Grace G   "   milliner.
"   Orson D   "   s
Gaskins Wm T, 253 Union n.   s
"   Fannie L   "   teacher.
Gavagan Andrew, 31 Griswold.
Geiger Eugene, 41   "   cook.
Gibbs Delia F, 29 South w.
Gier Frank M., M. D., office rooms 4, 5 and 6 over Goodrich's drug store. Office hours from 10 to 12 a m; 1:30 to 3 and from 7 to 8 p m.   Res 37 Broad.
Gier Hattie, 37 Broad s.
"   Henry, 1 Howell n, cooper.
"   Henry W, 80 South e, jus of peace.
"   Lydia, 80 South e.
"   Samuel J   "   teacher.
Gier & Haynes, fire insurance, real estate and collections, room 18 p. o. block, Hillsdale, Mich. H. W. Gier, justice of the peace and coroner. R. O. Haynes, county agent for the state board of corrections and charities and notary public.

Gr

Gifford Laura, 2 Howell n.
Gillett Daniel prop Gillett's hotel and dining hall. Rates $1.00 per day, single meals 25 cts. Everything first class, accomodating, cigars and fruits in the season. 1 Howell.
Gillett Anna, 213 Railroad e.
" Hannah, 120 Broad s.
" Laura M, 217 Railroad e.
" Mary, 111 Mead.
" Toney E, 213 Railroad e, laborer.
" Wm, 111 Mead, cooper.
Gilmore Samuel, 267 Bacon e, laborer.
Gilson Ella, 14 Howell s, merchant.
" Emma A, 9 McCollum, nurse.
Gilbert Marie, 52 West s.
" Mary, 57 West s, home bakery.
Globensky Louis, prop. cooperage works; factory and office Railroad e.
Globensky Etta, 119 Mead.
" Theresa "
Godden Harriette, 272 Railroad e.
" John "
Goodrich L. A. & Co. pharmacists and analytical chemists; a complete line of goods kept in the drug department. Prescriptions a specialty. 50 Howell n, res 60 Broad s.
Goodrich Mary A "
Gordon Lucy L, 374 Hillsdale n.
" Wm L " mason.
Gravner Wm. 236 Park, marble cutter.
Granger H B, 12 Bacon w.
" Rachel "
Gray C J, 122 Broad n, harness maker.
" Eveline, 46 West n.
" Fred " clerk.
" Hattie B "
" Justine " grocer.
Gray Justin, dealer in groceries; 112 Broad n. res 46 West n.
Gregg Hannah, 72 West s.
Green Bert F, 221 Hillsdale s.
Green E W, dealer in oil and gasoline; deliver to dwellings. The best grades of oil handled, only. res 221 Hillsdale.
" Frances R "
" George W, 221 Hillsdale. s.
" James O, Bacon w, lieut. U. S. A.
" Jennie "
" Lafayette W, 38 Reading av, fr.
" Lewis G, 11 Oak, laborer.
" " " clerk

Ha

Green, Lottie A, 116 Howder.
" Margarett, 38 Reading av.
" Sarah L, 11 Oak.
" Wm H, 116 Howder, printer.
Greene Fred, 54 Bacon w, printer.
" Nettie, 54 Bacon w, dressmaker.
Greenfield Ione, 245 Hillsdale.
Greening Anna. 118 Hillsdale, domestic.
Greenlee Chas N, 268 West n. s
Gregory Ann, 42 Howell s.
" Anna, 42 West n. s
" Anna, 105 Norwood av.
" Dora " domestic.
Grey E W, 276 West n. s
Griffin E. M, pastor of the Hillsdale Baptist church, rooms, 14 Manning s.
Griffith P, 300 West n.
Guernsey, A. L. attorney at law, chancery practice, Masonic block room 3. Residence 62 Waldron.
Guernsey Arthur L, 62 Waldron, atty,
" Edward " farmer.
Guggenheim Bertha G, 59 Broad s.
" Levi, 59 Broad s, merchant.
" Rosa "
Guggenheim L, merchant tailor and dealer in fine clothing and gents' furnishings. 84 Howell n, res
Guise Lizzie, 13 Howell s, dressmaker.
Gurney Chas H, 236 West n, coll prof.
" Mary R, 236 West n.
Guttenbergh Wm, 2 Howell n, bell boy.
Guy Carrie, 1 Howell, domestic.
Habel Mary, 17 West n, servant.
Hadley Cornelius, 5 Fayette e, Co. treas.
" Grant S, " teacher.
" Minerva, "
Hadley Nelson B., attorney-at law and justice of the peace; room 26 27 Waldron block; res. 5 Fayette.
Hadley Willard, 79 West s, teller.
Hagerman Charles B, 15 Norwood ave, sells machinery.
Hagerman Cordelia A, 15 Norwood ave.
" Fred E, "
Hagerty Allie, 348 Hillsdale.
Hall Mrs. Anna M., dressmaking parlors 9 howell s, room 24; all kinds of plain sewing, etc; res 9 howell s.
Hall Horace, 257 Union, farmer.
" Jane E, 41 Manning s.
" Lena, 75 Howell s.
" Marvin E, 75 Howell, merchant.

Ha

Hall, Mary L, 261 Union n.
" Rose, 2 Howell n, waitress.
Hallet Ada, 57 West s.
" Charles, 46 Short, machinist.
" Esther, 57 West s, home bakery.
" Pheba, 46 Short.
" Will, 57 West s, r r adv agt.
Hambel Fremont, 69 St. Joseph, laborer.
Hamblin Edward, Railroad w, cigar-mkr.
" Minnie, Railroad w.
Hamilton Chas, 34 Marion, cooper.
" Clara. 208 Hillsdale n, s.
" Emma, 34 Marion.
" Thomas, 104 Broad n, painter.
Hancock Carribell, 12 Howell n.
" Frank C, " clerk.
" Mary L, 5 Reading ave.
Hancock Oscar, dealer in Fancy and Staple groceries; 12 Howell n; res. 5 Reading ave.
Harrington Chas, 34 Garden, agri. agt.
" Charles, 67 South e, salesman.
" Loretta, 34 Garden.
" Leona, " saleslady.
" Nellie, "
" " 67 South e.
" N. W, 208 Hillsdale n, s.
Harris Charles, 49 Norwood ave s, lab.
" Eliza, Reading ave.
" Emma, 46 Reading ave.
" Eva, 46 Norwood ave s.
" Herbert, 46 Reading ave, r r bkm.
" Micazah, 238 Park, s.
" Sterling, 46 Reading ave. s.
" Thomas, "
Harris Dr. H., 13 Howell, Fisher block; office days Tuesday and Saturday afternoons; electric and water baths for the public; telephone to residence.
Harrison Ada, 58 West s.
Harvey Caroline, 66 Spring.
" Joseph, " farmer.
Hare Elizabeth, 37 Waldron.
Harkley Frank, 100 McClellan, wk. sc fc.
Harlan Lizzie, 70 North, domestic.
Harper Anna, 60 West s.
" George, "
" Rosella, "
Hammond Allen, 34 Manning n, ret. mer.
" Irene N, "
" Margaret, Mechanic e.
" Samuel, " laborer.
Hand Mary E, 98 Broad, domestic.

He

Handee Ella, 113 Oak, domestic.
Harding Geo D, 82 West n, county clerk.
" Louise, "
" Relief S, "
Haskins Alfred, 30 Short, work flour mill.
" Olive, "
Haskell Joseph, 77 State, farmer.
Haslem Nellie, 57 Railroad w.
" Wm, " r r emplee.
Hass John, 25 Marion, brewer.
Hathaway George L, 13 Howell s, clerk.
" Hannah, 252 West n.
" Julia A, 38 Railroad e.
" Laura, 13 Howell s.
Hathaway Leon, proprietor of tonsorial parlors under Smith house; shaving, hair-cutting and shampooing; res. 38 Railroad n.
Hauer Lydia E, 90 Howell s, domestic.
Hawes Delia M, 32 Railroad e.
Hawes Return P., proprietor of Cottage hotel, corner Railroad and Manning streets, (opposite depot); the only first class dollar a day house in city; electric light and steam heat in every room; single meals 25 cts; bath in connection; special rates to families.
Hayes Charles, Mechanic, laborer.
" Charles S, 248 Park, trav. salesman.
" Hannah, Mechanic.
" Irving, 8 Manning s, clerk.
" Margaret, 54 Spring.
" Maud, 8 Manning s.
" Vena, 248 Park.
Haynes Ann E, 100 Manning s.
" David, 361 Manning n, laborer.
" Frances, 191 Hillsdale, housekeepr.
" Frank, 361 Manning n.
" Frank J, 89 College e, photogphr.
" Joel B, 29 South w, retired famer.
" Julia, 361 Manning n.
" R. Orlando, 100 Manning s, ins. agt.
" Sarah, 29 South w.
" Sophia B, 191 Hillsdale, s.
Hazell Emma, 66 North, dressmaker.
Heie Amund O, 32 Railroad, tailor.
Helf Amelia S, 9 Lake, housekeeper.
Helmick Eli A, 38 Howell, lieut. U. S. A.
" Elizabeth A, 38 Howell s.
" Lotta, 2 Howell n, cook.
Heenan John C, 9 Manning n, carr'g mfr.
" Sarah C, "

Hi

Heenan Wm H, 9 Manning n, blacksmith.
Henry Amos, 225 Railroad e, laborer.
"   Sarah,   "
"   William D,   "   "
Hewey Julia, 2 Howell n, pastry cook.
Herrick Jas W, 102 Broad n, laborer.
Herring Anna, 85 Spring.
"   Gertrude,   "
"   Theodore,   "   engineer.
Hershey Ellen E, 205 Hillsdale.
"   Inez J,   "
"   Moses B,   "   mason.
"   Pearl,   "   teacher.
Herrin Harry, 235 Union n.
"   Harvey T.   "   ret. farmer.
"   Mary E,   "
Hervey James G, "   farmer.
Hettinger Harry V, 182 Bacon e, flour m'l.
Hewett Alexander, 21 South w, ret. farm.
"   Carrie,   "
"   Isabell, 83 Manning s.
"   Lewis K, 103 Sharp e, salesman.
"   Philander, 83 Manning s, ret farm.
Hews Lottie, 41 West n, domestic.
Hibbard Josephine, 8 Vine.
"   Robert D,   "   contractor.
Higbee Alberta, 75 Railroad w.
"   George H, 112 Mead, trav salsman.
"   Grace L, 198 Hillsdale n.
"   Herbert, 112 Mead, broom maker.
"   Jerome L, 198 Hillsdale n, minstr.
"   Julius, 75 Railroad w, r r employe.
"   Martha A, 198 Hillsdale n.
"   Mary R, 112 Mead.
Hill Edith W, 157 Hillsdale.
"   Elvira L, 205 Manning n.
"   Esther D, 237 Hillsdale.
"   Francis E, 205 Manning n, farmer.
"   Harriett K, 78 Reading ave, huskpr.
"   Millicent, 205 Manning n.
"   Nancy K, 187 Hillsdale, landlady.
Hilliker Charles, 206 Bacon e, painter.
"   Susan,   "
Hiller Arthur L, 29 Champaign, engineer.
"   Chas H,   "   s.
"   Ella, 32 Howell s.
"   Ellen B, 29 Champaign.
"   Hattie, 32 Railroad e.
"   Henry A, 29 Champaign, farmer.
Hillsdale Cigar Co., Ed M Franken-
stein, president; I J Frankenstein,
secretary and treasurer; cigar factory
No. 14 Howell.

Hu

Higgins Hattie, 59 Hillsdale, wrk in laun.
Hinkle Arthur, 51 Budlong, liveryman.
"   Bert E, 6 Vine,   "
"   Ernest, 43 North,   "
"   Lavena,   "
"   Nettie, 51 Budlong,   "
Hinkle Bros., livery, board and feed
stables, 55, 57 and 59 Broad n; baggage
and 'bus line; stylish turnouts at reas-
onable rates.
Hinkley Ada, 94 Manning s,
"   George R,   "   carpenter.
Hirsch Carl, 53 Monroe, r r employe.
"   Emma,   "
Hodges Charles, 15 Railroad w, r r fire.
"   Graham, 63 Oak, laborer.
"   Hannah, 12 Railroad w.
"   James,   "   laborer.
"   "   273 Bacon e,   "
"   John, 12 Railroad w,   "
"   "   286 Bacon e,   "
"   Mary, 63 Oak.
"   "   286 Bacon e.
"   Richard,   "   laborer.
Holden Edgar, 219 Railroad e, laborer.
"   Mary J,   "
Holdridge Alphonso, 115 Mead, brm mkr.
"   Ed, 120 Mead,   "
"   Elizabeth, 115 Mead.
"   Georgia, 120   "
"   Julia, 252 West n.
Holland J C, 245 Hillsdale,   s.
Holloway Sarah C, 98 West s.
Homan Abigail, 101 Manning s.
"   Charles,   "
Hopkins Harrison, 70 State, prop pat med.
"   Malinda,   "
Horrigan Jerry, 45 Monroe.
"   "   "   r r brakeman.
"   Kate,   "   domestic.
"   "   "   "
Houghton Zenith, 23 Marion, domestic.
Houtz Bertha, 116 Manning s, teacher.
"   Mariah,   "
"   Sherman W,   "   ret farmer.
Howard Matilda S, 59 Howell s.
"   Mary W,   "
Howe Jared 20 Howell s, grocer.
"   Jennie,   "   dressmaker.
Howland Edith, German.
Huckins Thomas, 93 Norwood ave, car mkr
Hufstader Mary, 8 Manning n.
"   W J   "   shoe mkr.

Jo

Hughes Clara L, 311 Hillsdale,   s.
Hughes E., physician, surgeon and oculist; special attention given to diseases of eye, ear and throat; also adjust glasses; office hours 1 to 2 and 6 to 7 p m.; office at residence 25 Broad.
Hughes Elizabeth, 311 Hillsdale.
"   Josephine A, 25 Broad s.
"   Wellington, 311 Hillsdale, florist.
Hueston Alexander, 40 Broad s, fire ins agt
"   John W,   "   clerk.
"   Latecia,   "
Hulce Alice, 272 West n.
"   Chas P,   "   s.
"   Clara M,   "   s.
"   Geo. W,   "   s.
"   Jennie,   "   s.
Huntley Margaret Railroad w.
"   Matthew,   "   huckster.
Hutchings Clayton, 1 Howell, carpenter.
Hutchins Addie, 84 College e,   s.
"   Lorinda,   "
Hyde Eva B, 36 Garden.
"   Hattie E,   "
"   Matthew,   "   plumber.
Ingersoll Cyrus, 363 Hillsdale n, farmer.
"   Harlow H   "   s
"   Ida S   "
"   Robert L   "   s
Irving Mary, 43 Howell s.
"   Paulus A, 43 Howell s, farmer.
Jackson Emma, 116 Mead.
"   Melvern   "   drayman.
Janes George A, 52 West s, city clerk.
"   Julia M, 78 West n.
"   Oscar A   "   attorney.
Jaesrich Chas S, 2 Howell n, cigar maker.
Jay Winnie, 81 West n.
Jennings Aaron, 232 West n.   s
"   Geo W, 98 Manning s, farmer.
"   Laura   "
"   Martin, 70 Howell, laborer.
Jerome Arthur, 57 Broad s, engineer.
"   Caroline   "
"   Horace   "   s
Johnson Dr C C, 186 Hillsdale n, phys.
"   Cynthia, 58 Manning n.
"   Edna, 153 Hillsdale, domestic.
"   Elizabeth, 2 Howell n.
"   Frank, 268 West n,   s
"   Fred, 55 Hillsdale.
"   Helen, 62 Howell, restaurant.
"   George, 55 Hillsdale, laborer.

Ke

Johnson Grace Y, 58 Manning n.
"   Jane, 55 Hillsdale.
"   Jelia B, 186 Hilldale n.
"   Jennie, 42 St Joseph, laundry.
"   John W, 124 Manning s, farmer.
"   Kate, 63 Oak.   s
"   Kate I, 65 Salem.
"   Kittie B, 55 Hillsdale.
"   Lizzie   "
"   Louise   "
"   Sallie, 124 Manning s.
"   Wallace, 65 Salem, tannery.
"   Wm J, r r fireman.
Jones Arvilla, 107 Manning s, teacher.
"   Edward S   "   drayman.
"   Henry, 72 Norwood av s, laborer.
"   Nancy R, 107 Manning s.
"   Onneey, 72 Norwood av s.
Jordan Geo T, 38 West n, law student.
"   Sadie M, 38 West n, teacher.
Joslin Edwin, 32 McClellan, blacksmith.
"   Eleanor S   "
Jowsey Hattie, 28 Ferris.
"   Rheuben   "   horseman.
Kahler Emma, 53 Hillsdale.
Kahler House, John Kahler prop, rates $1.00 per day; the best of accommodations furnished to patrons and the traveling public; board and lodging per week $3.50. 53 Hillsdale.
Kahler John, prop of Kahler House, 53 Hillsdale.
Kane Julia A, 12 Griswold.
"   Maggie, 27 Broad s, domestic.
"   Margaret, 64 Railroad w.
"   Mike, 12 Griswold.
"   Nelson, 7 Howell s, farmer.
Keating Andrew, 14 Railroad w, laborer.
"   Celia, 62 West n.
"   Elizabeth, 11 Railroad.
"   Joseph, 14   "   cigar maker.
"   Mary   "   "   dress maker.
"   Sarah   "   "   "
Keefer Andrew L, 89 Hillsdale, painter,
"   Benj, 217 West n, farmer.
"   Charles, 2 Howell w, hotel keeper.
Keefer Chas E, prop of the Keefer House.
Keefer House, rates $2.00 per day; appointments first class in every particular, electric light, steam heat.
Keefer Elmira, 41 Howell s.
"   Fred M, 131 West n, screen fac.

48   HILLSDALE CITY DIRECTORY.

Kl

Keefer Henry, 41 Howell s, farmer.
" Julia, 131 West n.
" Minnie B, 2 Howell w, landlady.
Keel Peter, 98 Broad, r r emp.
Kelley Alexander, 3 Monroe, r r clerk.
" Anna R, 2 Spring.
" Edward, 21 Ferris, laborer.
" Fred, 3 Howell, hackman.
" Genevieve, 116 Broad n.
" Emily, 3 Monroe.
" Levina, 21 Ferris.
" Mary, 2 Howell n.
" May Austin, 229 Union n.
Kellogg Minnie M, State, compositor.
Kempton Retta, 216 Manning n, teacher.
Kennan Albert L, 187 Hillsdale, minister.
" Belle R   "
Kendall Amos, 112 Howell s, salesman.
" Antinett   " s
" Florence   "
Kennedy Andrew, 10 Sharp w, cooper.
" Clara   "
" Burton S, Howell s, fruit grower.
" John P   " carpenter.
" Mary   "
Kenny Caroline, 281 Hillsdale.
" Moses P   " minister.
" Mary, 20 Ferris.
" Wm   " r r emp.
Kenyon Josephine, 94 Manning s.
King John F, 82 Broad s, farmer.
" Roxana P   "
Kingston Samuel, 212 Manning n, far.
" Vianea   "
Kinney Susie, 62 Manning s, teacher.
Kinyon D B, 96 Broad, meat market.
" Ella A   "   "
Kirby J Edward, 212 Manning n.   s
" Emily, 310 West n.
" Louisa   "
" Reuben S   " farmer.
Kirchner F, 139 Hillsdale, domestic.
Kirgoba Louisa, 257 South e.
Kitchen Wm, agt for the Singer mfg
company. Office in the Johnson block
opposite Smith's Hotel.
Kline John, 239 South e, laborer.
" Kate   " teacher.
" Maggie   " domestic.
" Margarett   "
Kline Geo J & Co, dry goods, cloaks
and carpets, 44 Howell n, res 19 Broad s.
Klemgert Adam, 232 South e, cig maker.

La

Klemgert May, 232 South e.
Kline Florence, 67 Budlong.
" George J, 19 Broad s, merchant.
" John W, 67 Budlong, painter.
" Maggie, 8 West n, servant.
" Mary M, 19 Broad s.
Knapp Florentine, 89 Mead.
" Frank L   " clerk.
" Frederick   " brakeman.
" Josephine   " dr maker.
" Louise A   " dr maker.
" Herbert, 49 West s, blacksmith.
" Nancy   "
Knickerbocker Geo A, 66 Howell, atty.
" Cornelia   " teacher.
Knickerbocker Geo A, attorney at
law, Masonic block Hillsdale Mich.
Kochenthal Bros & Co., clothiers.
Tailors and gents' furnishers; J Koch-
enthal, M Kochenthal, Rochester N Y;
M E Ollhausen, Hillsdale, Mich. Fac
tory and wholesale 82 N St Paul st,
Rochester N Y. 66 Howell n.
Koon Edith A, 46 Manning n.   s
" Lotta   "
Kohmer Elizabeth, 43 Monroe.
" John   " laborer.
" Manaka   "   "
" Martin   "   "
" Sarah   " domestic.
Krebbs Geo, 123 Broad n, cigar maker.
Kressbach John, 25 Railroad w, barber.
" Mary A   "
Krieter Lylia, 217 West n.
" Peter   " farmer.
Kromer Alice, 27 Ferris.
" Willie S   " r r eng.
La Fleur Asher B, 79 West s, cashier.
" Clara,   " s.
" Laura E,   " s.
Lake Mary A, 44 Fayette w.
Lamb Eliza, 91 Howell s.
" George, 225 Hillsdale,   s.
" May E,   " s.
" Morris, 91 Howell s, retired farmer.
Lambert George, 68 North, musician.
" Jane, 72 Spring.
" John, 273 Bacon e, meat market.
" Mary,   "
" Wm J, 72 Spring, gardner.
Lamereaux Edith H, 86 Howder.
" Peter R,   " gas fact.
Lamson David H, 52 Union, minister.

Le

Lamson Elizabeth, 52 Union.
" Mary E,   "   s
Lambert J. W., dealer in meats, vegetables, canned fruits etc; 74 Howell n.
Lana Luther M, Mechanic, brick maker.
Lancaster Chas E, 22 Budlong, r r clerk.
" Elizabeth,   "   mc teach.
" Morgan,   "   tinsmith.
" Ralph H,   "   s.
Landers Margaret, 41 Manning n, s.
Lane Anna, 182 Hillsdale n, teacher.
" Elizabeth,   "
" Roxana A, Mechanic.
Lane J. H., & Co., 44 McCollum, opp engine house. Pay highest market price for all kinds farm produce.
Langdon Elna, 45 Howell s.
" Henry,   "   merchant.
Langley Martha, 34 West s, tailoress.
Langworthy Clayton, 219 Manning n, s.
Lansing May, 182 Hillsdale,   s.
Lautsenbizer Lulu, 42 West n, servant.
Latchaw Chas F, 310 West n,   s.
Lawrence Albert H, Wolcott,   s.
" Charles E, 58 West n, merchant; see Lawrence & Co.
" Mary N, 58 West n.
Lawrence C. E. & Co, the old reliable hardware merchants. Sporting goods, cutlery, guns, fishing tackle, stoves, building material, mechanics' tools etc.
Laundry Bail's Steam, 44 St. Joseph; the best of work guaranteed; goods called for and delivered. Mrs. H. P. Bail prop.
Leader, The Hillsdale, published Fridays in Leader Building, Broad street. First class local paper. Republican in politics. E. J. March & Co.
Leavy Joseph J., ticket agent Lake Shore &Michigan Southern office; res. 17 Bacon w.
Leavy Carrie, 17 Bacon w.
Lee Fanny M, 77 Budlong.
Leggit John, 30 Howell, laborer.
Leland Caroline W, 9 McCollum, teacher.
Leman Clark, 27 Cemetery, laborer.
" Maggie   "
Lemmon Mary M, 75 Railroad w.
" Wilson   "   farmer.
Lester Jennie, 91 Sharp e.
" Robert   "   painter.

Ma

Lewis Alice A, 241 Hillsdale, teacher.
" Andrew W, 15 State, farmer.
" Anthony W, 69 Howell s, salesman.
" Bernice L, 85 Norwood av.
" Edward, 241 Hillsdale, minister.
" Eliza   "
" John W, 30 Griswold, laborer.
" Lucy H, 15 State.
" Myron, 85 Norwood av, r r emp.
" Senora, 241 Hillsdale, teacher.
" Violet L   "   s
" Wm H   "   s
" Viva, 69 Howell s.
Lige Alma V, 19 Monroe.
" Otis C   "   r r brakeman.
Lillibridge Cornelia, 81 College e.   s
Lincoln Arthur, 104 Manning s, salesman.
" Hattie   "
Locey Elmer, 150 Railroad w, line man.
" Sarah   "
Locklin Lysander L, 62 Manning s.
" Mary L   "
Lobnes Henry, 234 Bacon e, butcher.
" Lena   "
" Frances I, 14 Champaign.
" Henry C   "   butcher.
" John R   "   printer.
" May C   "   dressmaker.
" Wm H   "   farmer.
Lougher Ed H, 202 Manning n.   s
" Minnie W   "
Lord Emett A, 246 West n.
Love Eliza J, Barnard.
" John   "   laborer.
Lowell Charles, 84 Sharp e, laborer.
" Myra   "
Loyd Marie, 225 Hillsdale, dressmaker.
Luce Ella, 111 Railroad e.
" George   "   laborer.
Ludlam James, 45 Ludlam, furn dealer.
" Mabel   "
" Mercy   "
Lussenden E W, 216 Manning n.   s
Lyon Chas H, 94 College e.   s
" Genevieve   "   teacher.
" Mary E   "
" Emma 34 Howell s.
" Frank A   "   attorney.
" Mary D, 42 Manning n.
Madery Edw. C, 400 West n, work sc. fac.
" Julia J,   "
Maher Katie, 51 Spring.
" Philip,   "   tailor.

Mc

Maleolm Jesse, 101 Union,   tailor.
Malford Wm, 102 Broad n,   "
Maloney Caroline, 86 Budlong, milliner.
Maloney Miss Jettie B, modiste, 46 Bacon, south of Smith's hotel; res. 86 Budlong.
Mains Emma, Mechanic st.
Manning Maria, 228 Manning n.
Mausinberger Henry, 115 Fayette, farm.
" Mary E,   "
March Edwin J.; lawyer, editor and publisher of the Hillsdale Leader; postmaster Hillsdale office; res. 72 Manning n.
March Geo. K., city editor Hillsdale Leader; res. 72 Manning n.
March Sarah M.,   "
Marks Geo A, 205 Manning n, surveyor.
Marsh Adeline, German st.
" Edith M, 351 West n, stenographer.
" Embry, St Joseph, trav salesman.
" Eugene B, German, auctioneer.
" Herbert E, German.
" Jetur F,   "   retired farmer.
" Rosa A, St Joseph.
" Sara A, German.
Marshall Cloa, 40 Logan.
" Elijah H,   "   shoemaker.
" Fannie, 250 West n.   s.
Martin Cora, 20 Vine, teacher.
" Duncan, 312 Manning n, col. prof.
" George, 17 St. Joseph, barber.
" Hester, 312 Manning n.
" Hester M,   "
" Jean E,   "   artist.
" Robert,   "   teacher.
" Sarah, 17 St. Joseph.
" Wm T, 20 Vine, r r engineer.
Martindale Arthur, 15 Mechanic,   s.
" Orra,   "
Marvin Amelia C, 29 Manning s.
" Mary Jane,   "
Marx Lewis, 98 Broad, landlord.
" Sarah,   "
Mason Jane, 104 West s, dressmaker.
Maveety Patrick J., pastor of the Hillsdale Methodist church; res 41 Manning n.
Maxey Mary, 177 Manning n, teacher.
May Mary, 194 Bacon e.
" William J,   "   miller.
McBain Lenora, 46 Howell s, teacher.
McCabe Carrie, 24 Ferris.

Mc

McCabe John, 24 Ferris, r r laborer.
McClave Cordelia, 94 Broad.
" H P,   "   s.
McClave L H., home bakery; fresh bread, pies, cakes, etc.; finest lunch counter in the city; five doors north of Keefer house; 94 Broad n.
McClelland Chas B, 20 Vine, r r fireman.
" F B,   "   teacher.
" Lavira H,   "
McComb Henry, 73 Bacon e.
McConnell Alice, Baw Beese Park.
" Frank,   "   botmn.
McCune Thomas, 10 West s.
McDonald Henry F, 219 Manning n, s.
" John P, 85 College e.
" Mary,   "
McFadden Nora, 104 Manning s, servant.
McGuire Patrick, 53 Railroad w, r r emp.
" Rose,   "
McIntosh Anna, 33 Short.
" James,   "   plumber.
" Lydia,   "
" Nelson,   "   express driver.
McIntyre M, judge of probate and attorney at law, court house; res 32 Broad s.
McIntyre Mary L, 32 Broad s.
McKee Agnes, 174 Manning n, saleslady.
" Chas A, 25 Vine, carpenter.
" W, 11 West s, clerk.
" Grace,   "
" Jas, 174 Manning n.
" Jas W, 79 West n, clerk.
" John, 174 Manning n, clerk.
" Mary J, 79 West n.
" Mattie L,   "
" Sarah, 174 Manning n.
" Sarah L, 25 Vine.
McKercher Chas, at water works, eng.
" Sire B,   "
McLoughlin Clarence, laborer.
" Olive,   "
McManus Wm, 56 St Joseph, laborer.
McMasters Mamie, 30 Howell s.
McNair Ethel J, 239 West n, mc teacher.
" Frances M,   "
" Jessie G,   "   s.
" John O,   "   r r emp.
McNaughton F J, 220 West n,   s.
" Nettie B,   "   s.
McQueen James, 2 Sharp w, painter.
McReynolds Julia, 234 Manning n,   s.

Mo

McReynolds P W, 234 Manning n,   s.
McRitchie Emma A, 84 Union.
" Nellie I,   "   dressmaker.
" Wm,   "   farmer.
McSherry Eliza, 140 Broad s.
" William,   "   wk. flur mill
Mead H. P, & Co. dealer in crockery, china, solid silver and plated ware, cut glass, electric lamp goods, etc., 26 Howell n; res 58 West n.
Mead Homer P, 28 West, crockery merch.
Mead Louisa, 58 West n.
" Maria A, 155 Manning n.
" "   "
" Mary J, 85 Union.
Meek Lowell, 234 Manning n,   s.
Meffert Susie, 19 Broad s, domestic.
Merril Lucetta, 223 Manning n.
" Ira D,   "   farmer.
Metcalf John, 149 Howder, laborer,
" Minnie.
Merriman Mary, 15 Railroad.
Miller Anna, 16 West s, dressmaker.
" Carrie, 42 St. Joseph, wk in laundry.
" Eben P S, 221 Hillsdale,   s.
" Ida M, 1 Howell, waitress.
" Laura, 243 West n,   s.
" Lena, 16 West s, dressmaker.
" Mariah, 10 Broad s, domestic.
" Mary, 221 Hillsdale.
" " 1 Howell, waitress.
" Rosa, 152 Hillsdale, domestic.
" Samuel, 181 West n, wk. sc. factory.
" Wm H, 310 West n,   s.
Mitchell Charles T, 22 Manning n, bank.
" George, 34 West n. trav salesman.
" Harriett, 22 Manning n.
" Hortell, 34 West n.
Moeller August, 71 West s, cutter.
" Louise,   "
Mollis Mary, 84 Howell, clerk.
Montgomery Agnes T, 59 Howell s. nurse.
" Austin, 4 Railroad w, r r yardmaster
" Elizabeth,   "
" Minnie, 42 West s, r r clerk.
" Jas. 122 Broad, n, machinist.
" Julia F, 10 North.
" Nellie A,   "   teacher.
" Thomas C,   "   freight agent.
Montgomery William R. attorney and counsellor-at-law; especial attention given to drawing wills, contracts, leases and conveyances gener-

Mo

ally; to the investigation of titles to land and to the collection and foreclosures of notes and mortgages.
Moon Mary, 13 St. Joseph.
Moore Bernice, 22 West n.
Moore Dr. E. E. physician and surgeon; office over Boyle & Brown's store, Howell street; res No. 38 Manning n; office hours 10 to 12 a m, and 1 to 4 and 7 to 8 p m; telephone in residence.
Moore Emma, 89 German.
" Margaret W, 100 McClellan.
" Minnie, 38 Manning n.
" Nettie A, 181 West n.
" Samuel H,   "   trav salesman.
" Thomas E, 100 McClellan, fre sc fct.
" William, 89 German, laborer.
" Zephanial, 22 West n, physician.
More George, 59 Hillsdale, r r laborer.
" Lillie,   "
Morehouse Amy, 17 Norwood ave, n.
" Eliza, 46 Howell s.
" Isaac,   "   carpenter.
" Maude, 17 Norwood ave n, dressmkr.
" Silas.   "   teamster.
Morelock Catherine, 35 Short.
" Charles F,   "   millwright.
" Edward,   "   mail car.
" Fannie, 106 Sharp e.
" Frederick, 35 Short, teamster.
" George, 106 Sharp e, wk carge shop.
" William, 35 Short, teamster.
Morey Estella, 33 Broad s.
Morey F. E, D. D. S., office Guggenheim block, No 84 Howell, 2nd floor, front suit; res 33 Broad s.
Morgan Edwin M, 70 Manning s,trav sales.
" Fidelia,   "
" Leon, 2 Howell, clerk.
Morley Chester A, 50 Salem, wk sc fact.
" Ida,   "
" Mart J,   "   "
Morris Fatima, 47 West s.
" Mark,   "   trav salesman.
Mosher Ada J, 252 West n.
" Eleanor,   "
" Frances S, 230 "
" Frieda,   "   s.
Mosher George F., LL. D., President of Hillsdale College; res 230 West n.
Mosher Eugene T, 36 Short.
" George W,   "

Ne

Mosher Nellie, 36 Short.
" Stephen L,   "   clerk.
" George W, 122 Broad n, landlord.
" Jeanette,   "
" Sadie, 107 Manning s.
Moses Cora, 105 German.
" Fred,   "
" Hiram M,   "   carpenter.
" Mariah,   "
Moss Ira W, 102 Broad n, laborer.
Mowrey David T, Mechanic, laborer.
" George,   "   "
" John R, 246 West n, minister.
" Justina M,   "
" Hannah A, Mechanic.
Mullen Ben, Cemetery, cooper.
" Nancy,   "
" Ada,   "
" George,   "   cooper.
Mulqueen Harry, 9 Monroe, laborer.
" Margaret,   "
Munson Mary A, 234 Union.
" Wm H,   "   col prof.
Murdock Adelbert, 107 Budlong, carp.
" Augusta,   "
Murphy John, 37 Monroe, laborer.
" Luann, 100 Howell s.
" Margaret, 101   "
" Michael C, 37 Monroe, r r employe.
" Nora,   "
" Sebelle E,   "   compositor.
Murrey Manroy, 122 Broad n, domestic.
" Minerva, 86 Sharp e, cook.
" Wm, 122 Broad n, porter.
Myers Bertha I, 32 College e,   s.
" Delphine, 33 Howell s.
" Edith, 158 Hillsdale,   s.
" Florence L, 352 Manning n.
Myers Geo. W., "College Variety;"
"you can fool all of the people part the
the time and part of the people all of
the time, but you can't fool all the people
all of the time." You don't get fooled
at the Variety, 36 College; res same.
" Harry S, 32 College e,   s.
" Nancy B,   "
" William W, 33 Howell s, build cont.
Nash Orlando C, 236 Union n, teacher.
" Rhoda R,   "
Nelson Francis, 70 North, laborer.
Newcomer C L, 101 Hillsdale,   s.
Newman Carrie, 144 Railroad e.
" Wm J,   "   cooper.

O'M

Nichols Abigal, 306 West n.
" Anna,   "   s.
" Carrie S,   "
" Otto S,   "   s.
" Mary, 176 Manning n, florist.
" Sarah, 32 Railroad e.
Nickels Lena, 106 Sharp e, nurse.
Nicloy Nettie, Howell s, domestic.
Nimocks Anna A, 22 Garden.
" Geo O,   "   stone cutter.
Noble Wm A, 117 Hillsdale, upholsterer.
" Lena B,   "
Nobles Enas S, 211 Manning n, carpentr.
Norris Almeron, 62 Reading ave, farmer.
" Amelia,   "
" Chas S, 66 Barry, farmer.
" Clara M, 368 Hillsdale n.
" Edgar, 3 Howell s, peddler.
" Elnora, 83 South e.
" Hellen J, 62 Reading ave,   s.
" Joel B, 66 Barry, comm'r of poor.
" Mary, 3 Howell s.
" Mary C, 66 Barry.
" Seth N, 368 Hillsdale n.
" Susan B,   "
North Walter H, 219 Manning n,   s.
Northrup Albert, 113 College e, farmer.
" Mary A,   "
Northway Charles, 207 Griswold, painter.
Norton Carrie, 25 Broad s, domestic.
Noyes Henry, 98 Norwood ave, draym'n.
" Mary,   "
Null Alice, 61 Broad n.
" Willie,   "   teamster.
Nuly Marie, 62 Howell, domestic.
Nutten Fally, 234 Manning n.
Oberlin Charlotte, 45 Mechanic.
" Henry   "   clerk.
O'Brien Homer, 268 West n.   s
Oesterle John M, 99 Budlong, tailor.
" Thekla   "
Ollhausen Isaac, 2 Howell, merchant.
" Max E, Keefer House. See Kochenthal Bros. & Co.
O'Meara Daniel, 68 Howell, laborer.
" Kate   "   milliner.
" Matthew   "   elec line man.
" Daniel L, 61 Oak, laborer.
" Ellen P   "
" John   "   painter.
" Ella R, 19 Oak
" Wm   "   painter.
" Louise, 71 Oak

Pa

O'Meara Mat D, 71 Oak.
O'Niell Bessie, Howell n.
Oppel George, 84 St Joseph, carpenter.
" Renata "
Orcutt Elizabeth, 97 Manning s.
Osburn Edgar W, 47 Cemetery, farmer.
" Nora "
Otterson Martha, 42 West s.
Our H Irene, 246 West n. s
Overn Alonzo, 64 West s, horseman.
" Zoe "
" Edith, 4 West n, servant.
Owen Walter I, 2 Howell n, Sec Gas Co.
Paine Stella, 14 Railroad.
Painter Frank, River e, laborer.
" Mary "
Palmer Betsy, 102 West n, domestic.
" Elizabeth, 161 Manning n, drmaker.
" Jas D, 118 Hillsdale, contractor.
" Sophronia "
Palmer Julian A., notary public and real estate agent. Room 15 Waldron block; res 148 Manning n.
Palmer Kate, 148 Manning n.
" Lizzie T " s
Pardee Caroline A, Fayette w.
" John W " farmer.
Parkinson Clara, 148 Railroad w.
Parker Chas W, 63 Sharp e, salesman.
" Harriett M, 12 Sharp w.
" Howard, 208 West n. s
" Ida H, Bacon w.
" J Bartlett, 12 Sharp w, stone mason.
" John S, Bacon w, see Fredonia Washer Co.
Parker Mina L, 63 Sharp e.
" Wm, 203 Bacon w, gardener.
Parkhurst Emma, 86 Bacon w.
" Emma L. 55 West s.
" Frank W " grocer clerk.
" John C, 86 Broad w, teamster.
" Lewis E, 55 West s, grocer. See Parkhurst & Ranney.
Parks Geo A, Montgomery, laborer.
" Maria E "
" Martha M "
Parmelee Alonzo, 17 Champaign, farmer.
" Ellen L "
" Ezeriah, 95 Broad s.
" Francis D, 18 Reading av, mecht.
" Horatio, 58 Manning n, geologist.
" Jennie "
" Linus " s

Pi

Parmelee Mary S, 18 Reading av.
Parmelee J., watchmaker and manufacturing jeweler, with W. L. Stone dealer in watches, jewelry, clocks, optical goods, etc; 65 Howell n; res 18 Reading av.
Parsons E M, 276 West n, minister.
" Minnie "
Partridge John, 37 Norwood av s, pntr.
" Myrta E, "
Poskit Thomas, 82 State, laborer.
Patton Frank C, 26 St Joseph, dep p m.
" Lela A " dressmaker.
" Mary E "
Paul Elmina, 90 German.
" Trumau " carpenter.
Pavey Alice, 83 Hillsdale.
Payne Chas J, 32 Sharp e, brick mason.
" Lucy E "
Perry Carrie L, 88 Manning s.
" Wm P " mail carrier.
" Fred, Union, clerk.
" George " grocer clerk.
" Herbert " tel line man.
" Kate A "
" Mary W, 114 Hillsdale.
Peters Ann M, 93 Howell s.
" May "
" Thos W " salesman.
Peterson Ambrose, 21 Manning n.
" Iva "
" May, 218 Hillsdale n. s
Petrie Agnes, 28 West s, clerk.
" Ida E "
" Wm " "
Pettit Minnie, 48 College e. s
Petyt John, 62 St Joseph, photographer.
" Mary "
Phelps Homer E, 6 College w. s
" Josiah " teacher.
" Mary A "
" Myrta M " mus teacher.
Phibbs Thomas, 122 Broad n, cig maker.
Phillips Emma, Railroad w.
" Frank W " farmer.
Phlyn Caroline, 64 Spring.
" Daniel " r r fireman.
Pierce Albert H, Manning s.
" Edwin K, 2 Howell n, clerk.
" George, 31 Manning n, salesman.
" Helen, 31 Manning n.
" Lodema " s
" Saretta " n

Ra

Pierce Hiram, 122 Broad n, carpenter.
Platter, 62 Howell, agent.
Playford George, 37 St Joseph, sh maker.
" Lydia A   "
Plum Josephine, 28 Marion.
" Sylvester   "
" Wm   " laborer.
Pond Julia A, 3 Manning n.
Porter Almeda, 206 Ellen.
" Christopher   " wagon maker.
" Ester, 46 West n, clerk.
" John E, 43 Oak, carriage maker.
" Phoebe O   "
Post Eliza K, 47 Budlong.
" Stillman W   " farmer.
Powers Anna, 76 Spring, milliner.
" Catherine   "
" Nellie   " dressmaker.
" Wm   " brakeman.
Pratt Mary, Bacon w.
" Daniel L " lawyer.
Prentiss Adelaide, 215 Manning n.
" Mary C   "
" Albert B, 2 West s, farmer.
" Harriett   "
" Frank W, 17 West n, bank cashier.
" Myrtle   "
Prideaux Ada, 65 Howell s, clerk.
" Emma   "
"   "   "
" George D   " wheat buyer.
" Minnie   "
Proctor Frank K, 38 Budlong.
" Rilla   "
" Nancy, 243 Union n.
" Samuel D   " mason.
" Sarah F   "
Pulsifer Arvilla, 243 West n.
" Sam J   " carpenter.
Pulver William, 100 McClellan, scr fac.
Parkhurst & Ranney, Lewis Parkhurst; Everett Ranney; dealers in groceries, provisions and feed; 41 Broad n.
Randell Jeddie, 92 Hillsdale, tinner.
Randolph Amanda, 33 Champaign.
" Anna L, 231 Hillsdale,   s.
" Margaret,   " teacher.
" Sophia,   "   s
" Benjamin, 10 Bacon e, farmer.
" Lucy A,   "
" Chas F, 33 Champaign, blacksmith.
" Clovis T, 352 Hillsdale n, labr.

Re

Randolph Loring E, 352 Hillsdale n.
" Viola,   "
Ranney Caroline, 102 Howell s.
" Everett L,   " grocer. (see Parkhurst & Ranney.)
" Lemuel S, 267 Bacon e, farmer.
" Margaret G,   "
Ransier Anna C, 89 Hillsdale.
" Wm,   " r r clerk.
" Mary, 92 Sharp e.
" Fred,   " drug clerk.
" Frank, 84 South e, laborer.
" Ella,   "
" John, 39 Norwood ave s, drayman.
" Elizabeth,   "
" George, 230 South e, laborer.
" Jennie,   "
Rapp O S, 191 Hillsdale,   s.
Rayner Eunice, 41 Welch.
" Jas S,   " laborer.
Rayney Albert, 146 River e, farmer.
" Edith E,   "
" Melvin J, 15 Fayette w, scr'n factry.
" Myrtie,   "
Reed Amy, 52 Budlong.
" Job,   "
" Delevan B, 48 College e, col. prof.
" Martha J,   "
" Harriet G, 78 Reading ave.
" Jenna, 63 Marion.
" Thomas, 52 Budlong, carpenter.
" Wm,   " butcher.
Reihorn Carrie, 28 Monroe.
" Charles,   " cigar maker.
Reiley Louise, 68 West n.
" Marian,   " teacher.
" Mary C,   "
" Sarah M,   " teacher.
Remaly Mose, Cemetary, laborer.
Rennison, H. T., harness maker; carry everything in the harness line; harness made to order; robes, blankets, whips, etc; 48 Broad n; res. 115 West n.
Reynolds Electa F, 219 Manning n.
" Elon G, 220 Manning n, col. treas.
" Emily B,   "
" Emma G, 300 West n.
" H W,   " fire and life ins.
Reynolds Lorenzo P., Insurance; best companies; leading agency; 15 years experience and every loss paid; office over Frisble's grocery, No. 8. Here to stay; res 219 Manning.

Ro

Rennison Ada R, 26 Oak.
Ribbeck Christina, 91 Howder.
" Fred " tailor.
" George A, " printer.
" Andrew G, "
Ricaby Harriet A, 131 Manning s.
" Julia B, " clerk.
" Sanford, " agt. theatrical co.
Rice Armida, 84 Manning s.
" Levi J, "
" Levi Bert, 100 Hillsdale, r r emp.
" Anna E, "
" Orval N, " salesman.
" Lenna M, " s.
" Leota A, "
" Charles, 32 College e, s.
" Louisa, 136 Manning s.
" Ned A, " laborer.
Richardson Mattie, 114 Broad n, teacher.
Rideout Alexander C, Principal
of Commercial and Telegraphic Dep't.
Hillsdale College. Shorthand, tele-
graphy, book-keeping, etc.
Riehm Geo J, 31 Union, (under car'g mfr.)
" Mary L, "
" Mary M. "
Rigden Bert N, 34 College e, groc. clerk.
" Verna, "
Riggs Clara B, 115 West n.
" Diana, 21 Railroad.
" Ed, 122 Broad, produce merchant.
" Orrin J, 115 West n, carpenter.
" Valentine, 21 Railroad, laborer.
Riker Harriett W, 199 Bacon e.
" Geo K, " laborer.
Riley Borbritt, 207 Union n, domestic.
" Ed, 63 Railroad w, teamster.
" Anna, "
" John, " laborer.
" Kate, " dressmaker.
" Rose, "
Rippon Maria R, 148 Hillsdale.
" Thomas, . " supt tel.
Risedorph Martha, 84 McCollum.
" Orlando H, 84 McCollum, lum deal.
" Sarah A, "
Rising John, 16 West n, retired farmer.
" Lurane, "
" Myron H, " salesman.
Robertson Alvira, Howell s.
" Arthur, " farmer.
" Ed, 122 Broad n, hotel clerk.
" Harley D, 81 Broad s, trav salesman.

Ru

Robertson Mary J, 38 Railroad e, dom.
" Nellie G, 81 Broad s.
Roby Agnes A, 12 College w, dressmaker.
" Cordelia, "
" Edward, " farmer.
" Edwin S, " drayman.
" Giles, " clerk.
" Martha A, "
" Norman, " drug clerk.
Robinson Jesse P, 245 Hillsdale, s.
Rogers Carrie M, 37 Manning n.
" Eli B, " farmer.
" George, 106 Norwood ave, teamster.
" Harry J, 104 Hillsdale, miller.
" Hattie, 106 Norwood ave.
" Jessie, 37 Manning n.
". Mary E, 104 Hillsdale.
Root Harriette L, 87 West n.
" James A, " r r condctr.
" James W, " farmer.
" Mary B, "
" Sarah E, "
Rose Charles, 122 Broad n, r r brakeman.
" Judson A, 98 Oak, photographer.
" Lillian, "
Rossiter Samuel 61 Salem, laborer.
Rowley Ella M, 72 Budloug.
" Marilla, "
Rowley Martin V. B., jeweler and
watchmaker; everything usually kept
in a first-class jewelry store; engraving
and fine watches; 71 Howell n; res. 72
Budlong.
Rowlson Charles H, 15 West n.
" S Clark, (see Rowlson & Son) 62
West n, editor.
" Harvey B, (Rowlson & Son) 62
West n, editor.
" Polly A, 15 West n.
" Rowena, 76 Budlong.
Rowlson & Son, editors and proprie-
tors of the Hillsdale Standard (see
Standard); office 42 Howell n, 2nd
floor.
Ruckman Edward, 42 West n, clerk.
Ruggles Darwin D, Manning s, farmer.
Ruggles G. M., mfr. of marble and
granite monuments; rustic and marble
stone, etc.; office 72 Bacon e; res. 120
Manning s.
Ruggles Margaret, Manning s.
" Mary, 120 Manning s.
Rupright Ida, 50 Howell s, wk photo gal.

Sc

Russell Chas E, 4 Railroad w, undertkr.
" Clarence S, 32 Broad s.
" Ida, "
" James, 68 West s, laborer.
" Jennie E, 84 Budlong, dressmaker.
" Jessie L, 4 Railroad w.
" Kate A, 32 Broad s.
" Minnie L, " probate register.
" Olive C, 475 West n.
Sackett Maggie, 13 Broad s, domestic.
Salley Rev. Ashmun T., A. M., D. D., pastor of Free Will Baptist church; Dunn professorship of Hebrew language and literature; res 153 Hillsdale.
Salley Ellen C, "
Salmon Elizabeth, 240 West n, s.
Samm Burt L, 8 Bacon w.
" Ella, 57 Broad n.
" Herbert W, 8 Bacon e, grocer.
" Lucy A, "
Sampson Bessie, 72 West s, teacher.
" Henry W, " carpenter.
" Isabell, "
" Maranda, 54 Bacon w.
" Mary, 26 Bacon w.
" Mary A, 6 North, domestic.
" May, 26 Bacon w.
Sampson W. J., attorney-at-law; rooms 20 and 21, Waldron block; res 26 Bacon w.
Sands Claire, 268 West n, s.
" L L, "
Saunders Sarah, 176 Manning n, dresmkr.
Saviers Jennie, 30 State.
Sawyer Harriett M, 12 Manning n.
Sawyer Walter Hulme, M. D., office Commercial block; hours 1 to 4 p. m.; 28 Howell n, 2nd floor, front suite; res. 12 Manning n.
Saxton John C, German, painter.
" Mary J, "
Sayles Alice, 162 Manning n.
" Charles, " clerk.
" Emma L, " accountant.
" Herbert L, " tinsmith.
" Horace E, " minister.
" Lucy B, " tel operat.
" Sadie L, " mus teacher.
Scanlon Daniel, 39 Bacon w, laborer.
" Michael, 2 Howell n, hotel clerk.
Schafer George, 79 Hillsdale, r r brake.
" Henry, 65 Hillsdale, r r clerk.
" Kate M, " "

Se

Schafer Mary, 63 Hillsdale.
" Mary D, 79 Hillsdale.
Scheick John, German, cooper.
Shicks George, 122 Broad n, butcher.
Schmidt Carlie, 45 West n, domestic.
" Charles, 213 South e, laundry.
" John, " blacksmith.
" Kate, 22 Manning n.
" Kate, 213 South e.
" Mary, 314 Bacon e.
" Mina, 48 Union.
Schovel Sarah, 122 Broad n, domestic.
Schults Julia A, 96 Broad s.
" Theodore, " fisherman.
Schwartz Franc, 100 Broad s.
" Fred, " laborer.
Scott Edwin, 16 West s, mason.
" Emeline, "
" Lottie, " s.
" Nellie, 66 North, milliner.
Sears Albert W, 76 College e. s.
" William T, " s.
Seeley Nancy A, 89 North.
" Robert, " dyer.
Segner Agnes A, 195 Bacon e, teacher.
" George L, " tailor.
" Mary A. "
" Orland B, " r r fireman.
Seidell Amelia, 36 Howell n.
" Christiane, 3 Broad s.
" William T, 36 Howell n, baker.
Seiler Galem, 50 Manning s, clergyman.
" Mary E. "
Seitz Elise, 41 Griswold, clerk.
" Elizabeth, "
" Fred H, " tel operator.
" Mary, " tailoress.
Seitz Robert, stationer, newsdealer and general subscription agent, 53 Howell n; mngr. Western Union telegraph office; office 59 Howell n, 2nd floor; res. 41 Griswold.
Selden Ann M, 202 Union n.
" Geo W, " farmer.
" May L, 202 Union n, s.
Sellers Albert, 41 Howell s, kpr sum res.
" Emma, " pastry cook.
" Frank, "
" Mike E, 8 Railroad, laborer.
" William, 2 Howell n, restauhelp.
Seney Minnie, 198 Bacon e.
" Seymour, " (see Seeney & Van Riper), machinists.

KOCHENTHAL BROS. & CO., Leading Tailors in Southern Michigan. Popular Prices, Immense Stock, First Class Work Only.

HILLSDALE CITY DIRECTORY. 57

Sh

Seney & VanRiper, S. Seney, F. Van Riper, proprietors of Hillsdale Iron Works; jobbers in machinery, foundry and brass supplies; all kinds of machine repairing done; prices reasonable; office 43 Ferris n.
Serbert Thomas, 3 Howell, laborer.
Shafer Carato, 36 Bacon e.
" Frank, 77 Howder, laborer.
" George W, 40 West n, mail carrier.
" Gilman B, 104 Broad s, tailor.
" Harriett M, 40 West n.
" Mary A, 104 Broad s.
" Mary L, 77 Howder.
Shanks Persia, 39 Bacon w.
" Sylvester J, " mkt gardner.
" Will Mortimer, " gardner.
Shaw Harriett M, 84 Howell, dressmaker.
" Mary J, 230 South e.
" Merritt, 103 Budlong, carpenter.
" William W, 230 South e, fireman.
Sheldon Annie E, 320 West n.
" Benj E, " jus of peace.
" Cora, 52 West n.
Sheldon C. H., dealer in boots and shoes, gloves and mittens and rubber goods, 22 Howell n, res. 52 West n.
Sheldon Edna, 320 West n.
" Emma, 66 Manning s.
" Henry, " clerk.
" Mae, 52 West n.
Shepard Chas A., attorney-at-law; office 15 Waldron block; res. 77 Budlong.
Shepard Flora A, 76 Fayette e.
" Ida A, 77 Budlong.
" Joseph W, 76 Fayette e, cab maker.
" Lida, 77 Broad s.
" Mary E, 76 Budlong.
Sheriff Caroline, 95 Manning s.
" Charles, 2 Howell n, upholsterer.
Sherman Patience, 212 Manning n.
Shields Gertrude, 60 Broad s.
Shiner John, 140 River e, farmer.
" Nancy, "
Shoemaker Henry, 19 Champaign, cooper.
" Wm, " "
Showers Elizabeth, 31 McClellan.
" Margaret, " wk sc fac
Shuart Carrie E, 12 West n.
Shuart W. L., superintendent of Hillsdale public schools; res. 12 West n.
Shultz Albert, 81 Howder, r r employe.

Sm

Shultz Anna, 63 Marion.
" Charlotte, 50 West s.
" Christopher, 63 Marion, carpenter.
" Ella, 81 Howder.
" Eva M, 63 Marion.
" Fred H, "
" Hiram, 50 West s, laborer.
Shults John, 62 Howell, coachman.
Sidell Ed, 32 Railroad e, tel operator.
Silk Harry, 104 West s, pickle manufr.
" Lucy N, "
Simms Robert P, 248 Park, s.
Sinclair Julia, 221 Union n.
Singer Cortes E, 96 Howell s, furn dealer.
" Myra E, "
Sims Hiram, 148 Howder, laborer.
Skiff Ferdinand, German, teamster.
" Minerva, "
Slack Geo H, 48 Norwood ave w, tic agt.
" Ella M, "
Slane Rev. Father P. J., pastor of St. Anthony's Roman Catholic church; res. 11 Broad s.
Slashing Louisa, 257 South e.
" Paul, " cooper.
Slaybaugh Anna, 245 West n, s.
" L S, " s.
" Martha, " s.
Smith Abbie G, 20 Railroad.
" Abigail J, 80 Howder.
" Amelia, 6 Bacon e.
" Charles, 53 Howell, coal dealer.
" Charles A, 201 Manning n, merch.
" Charles H, 6 Bacon e, druggist.
" Clara L, 119 Howder.
" Clarence, 182 Hillsdale n.
" Cornelia, 41 Broad s.
" Cyril B, 201 Manning n, clerk.
" Edward, 95 Broad s, horse trainer.
" Edward J, 2 Howell s, livery fore.
Smith E. J., dealer in groceries, 53 Howell n; res. 41 Broad s.
Smith Elizabeth, 23 Monroe.
" Ella, 64 Norwood ave s.
" Ellen L, 4 Fayette e.
" Ellen W, 211 Manning n.
" Emma K, 114 Howell s.
" Emma V, 6 Bacon e.
" Etha M, 4 Fayette e, s.
Smith Eugene, teacher of music and dancing; the latest Detroit and Chicago dances; res. 20 Railroad e.
Smith Florida, 94 West s, s.

Sm

Smith Frank, 10 Railroad w, r r engineer.
" Frank W, 114 Howell s, trav sales.
" Fred W, 41 Broad s, musician.
Smith Geo. N., 78 Howell; general hardware; hot air, steam and hot water heating a specialty; plumbing and agricultural implements: sporting goods of all kinds; res. 119 Howder.
Smith Geo W, 64 Norwood ave s, scr fac.
" Harriett, 26 Railroad.
" Helen H, 201 Manning n.
" Henry, 25 Vine, laborer.
" Henry B, 80 Howder, farmer.
" Henry E, 27 Railroad, cab maker.
Smith House, A B Dickinson prop; rates $2.00 per day; appointments in every particular first-class; steam heat and all other modern conveniences.
Smith Ida, 9 St. Joseph.
" Jane, 22 Fayette w.
" Jessie B, 2 Spring.
" John H, 62 Howell, cooper.
" John W, 72 North, laborer.
" Joseph, 115 Howder,   s.
" Juliett, 14 Budlong.
" Kittie, 182 Hillsdale n.
" Lelia'I, 211 Manning n, mus teacher.
" Leroy A, 26 Railroad, cab maker.
" Levi, 2 Howell n, clerk.
" Lillian, 59 Howell s.
" Louise, 10 Railroad w.
" Louis, 74 Broad s, laborer.
" Louise, 115 Howder.
" Lyda, 15 Monroe, seamstress.
" Martin, 80 Howder, laborer.
" Mary, 15 Monroe.
" Mary, Bacon e.
" Mary, 224 Manning n.
" Mary E, 119 Howder.
" Mary E, State.
" May, 76 Manning s.
" Milla, 2 Howell s.
" Nettie, 13 Short.
" Nicholas, 2 Spring, r r employe.
" Oliver, 13 Short, cooper.
" Orla, 22 Fayette w, laborer.
" Pheba J, 72 North.
" Rhoda E A, 114 Howell s, evangelist.
" Rose, 37 Waldron, dressmaker.
" Sarah, 76 Manning s, seamstress.
" Seth H, 4 Fayette, farmer.
" Shirley H, 201 Manning n, sec Y W C A.

St

Smith Shiloh, 211 Manning n,   s.
" Thomas, 15 Monroe, cigar maker.
" Thomas G,   "   laborer.
" Thomas S, 76 Manning s, cooper.
" Verne, 201 Manning n,   s.
" William, 9 St Joseph, cooper.
" Wm C, State, harness maker.
" William H, 15 Monroe, laborer.
Smith W. H. & Bros, dealer in carriage horses; livery and coach to all trains; connected with Smith's hotel; dealers in wagons; office and barns 42 Bacon e.; res. 2 Howell s.
Smithpeter Franck, 237 South e.
" John,   "   laborer.
Snyder Belle, 33 Manning s.
" Ezra E, 31 St Joseph, miller.
" John C, 33 Manning s, dentist.
" Maggie, 31 St Joseph.
Sparks George, 72 Ferris.
" Lena, 186 Manning s, dressmaker.
" Millie, 72 Ferris.
Sparrow Geo, 29 Short, laborer.
" Henry,   "   machinist.
" Mary,   "
Speer Andrew J, 35 Manning s, prod mr.
" Frank H,   "   engineer.
" Sarah,   "
Spencer Blanche, 221 Union n,   s.
" Genevieve,   "   s.
" James M, 29 Broad n, r r brakeman.
" Lelia E, 101 Reading ave.
" Maggie, 29 Broad n.
" Norris A, 101 Reading ave, drayman.
" Roxy, 29 Broad n, dressmaker.
Sperbeck Ellen, 66 Spring.
Sprague Frank, 125 Railroad, wk tannery.
" Nina, 186 Hillsdale, domestic.
" Sadie, 125 Rairoad w.
Spiegel August C, 66 Broad s, restaurant.
" Edward,   "   exp driver.
" Linda,   "   tailoress.
" Louisa,   "   milliner.
" Margaret,   "
Springstead Florence N, 83 German.
" Lyman,   "   mason.
" Thomas J,   "   "
Squier Caroline, 89 Oak.
" Lem E,   "   merchant.
Stage Asa T, 45 River, laborer.
" Frank G,   "   "
" Henry C,   "   "
" Margaret,   "

St

Standard, The Hillsdale, office 42 Howell n, 2d floor; H B Rowlson & Son, publishers and proprietors; established in 1840; circulation 2,100; best equipped job office in southern Michigan; republican in politics.

Stafford Angie F, 208 Hillsdale n.
" Ellen, 11 Broad n, housekeeper.
" Mary E, 20 Manning n.
" Orsell C, " agt Stand Oil Co.
" Sadie M, 208 Hillsdale, wk tannery.

Stahl John A, 22 Marion, peddler.
Stanfield Ada, 9 North, domestic.
Stanley Joel, 151 Spring, farmer.
Stanton Ella L, 101 Union.
" Frank M, "
" Mary, 151 Spring.
" Anna E, 115 Howder.
" Gilbert J, " farmer.

Steele May E, 81 College e, s.
Stephens Emma, 16 Railroad.
" Matthew, " brmmaker.
Stevens Clara, Bacon w.
" Clarance, " laborer.
Stevenson Delia A, 228 Manning n.
" Susan, 21 Railroad w.
" Wm. " r r employee.
" Wm F, 228 Manning n, carpenter.

Stewart Addie, 9 Garden.
" Carrie E, 6 North.
" Charles F, " bank cashier.
" E G R, 230 West n.
" E J, 6 Railroad, express agent.
" Elizabeth, 36 Manning s.
" Ellen, 6 Railroad.

Stewart F. M., president of First National bank of Hillsdale; res. 36 Manning s.

Stewart Wesley, 9 Garden, painter.
Stiles Jennie T, 252 Union n, s.
St John Clara, 224 West n, s.
Stimson Belle, 140 River e, work tannery.
" Emma, " "
" Sarah, 140 Howder, "

Stock Adolph, 29 Broad s, clerk.
" Alex, 40 Manning, bookkeeper.
" Emma C, "
" Fred W, 3 Broad s, trav salesman.
" Frederick W, " flour manufactr.
" Marguerite, 29 Broad s.
" Minna, 3 Broad s.

Stoddard Adolph, 21 Ferris, wagonmkr.
" Carrie, 2 Howell n, pastry cook.

St

Stoddard Elizabeth, 21 Ferris.
Stone Anaretta, 124 Manning s.
" Bert, 77 State, r r fireman.
" Caroline, 2 Sharp w.
" Delmer E, State, laborer.

Stone Fred H., attorney-at-law; office, room 25 Waldron block; res 9 North.
Stone Geo A, 70 North, cigarmaker.
" George C, " mason.
" Harriet, "
" Helen C, 99 Union.
" Hellena, 59 West s.
" Jennie, 65 State.
" Madora, "
" Mary E, 70 North.
" Minnie, 2 Sharp w.
" Roscoe, "
" Thomas, "
" Will, 59 West s.
" Wm J, 65 State, city marshal.
" Wm L, 99 Union, jeweler.

Storms August, 92 West n, r r trckmastr.
" Elizabeth, "
" John W, " r r clerk.

Story May, 35 Manning n, servant.
Stowell Herman D, 387 Hillsdale, teacher.
" Jas M, 351 West n, farmer.
" Mary L, "
" Hattie M, 387 Hillsdale, teacher.
" Millie A, "
" Orvis D, "

Straight Marian, 292 Hillsdale n.
Stratton Lama A, 110 St Joseph.
" William N, " laborer.
Straub John, 24 Garden, r r employe.
" Mary Ann, 112 Howder.
" Orburn, "
" Sarah, 24 Garden.

Straw Ina L, 16 Mechanic, s.
" Roy, 16 Mechanic.
Strayer Bert, 102 Broad n, painter.
" Viola, 102 Broad n, domestic.
Strickland Alveda, 230 Manning n.
" F G, " s.
" George, 122 Broad n, laborer.
Sueen Harriett, 2 Howell, chambermaid.
Strunk George H, 28 Vine, carpenter.
" Jane, 34 West n.
" Rose, "
" Samantha, 28 Vine.

Stull Albert E, 22 Marion, wagon maker.
" Mattie R, "
" Rebecca, 12 Spring.

Th

Sullivan Catherine, 81 Budlong.
" Timothy, "
Sutfin ———, 66 State.
Sutherland John, 32 Railroad e, clerk.
Sutton Anna W, Railroad w.
" Benj, " carpenter.
" Gertrude, 32 Manning n.
Sutton John R, insurance agent; nothing but old line companies represented; loan and real estate office, 32 Howell n; res 32 Manning n.
Sutton Mary E, Railroad w.
" Matilda, "
Swartz Christina, 108 Howder.
" Gotlieb, " laborer.
Sweet Margaret, 82 State, domestic.
Swell Deloss, 122 Broad n, mill wright.
Swift Jay, 2 Howell, pharmacist.
Tafner Amelia, 83 west s.
" Volney, " tailor.
Tallman Chas, 32 West s.
" Wm H, " printer.
" Cora, "
Taylor Carrie A, 64 Union, milliner.
" Julia M, "
" Wm, " printer.
" Josephine, 62 West n.
" Lucy, 83 West n.
" Mart W, 83 West n, harness maker.
" Theodore, " s.
Teall Ada, 2 Howell n, domestic.
Terpening Amanda C, 120 Howell s.
" Lucas H, "
Terwilliger Annives, 111 Howder, carp.
" Callie, "
" Clarence, " decorator.
" Jane "
Thatcher Charles L, 35 Manning s. (see Thatcher & Son, booksellers)
. " Sophia, 35 Manning s.
" Fred, 33 Manning s, bookseller, (see Thatcher & Son)
" Mabel, 33 Manning s.
Thatcher C L & Son, dealers in books, stationery and wall paper; 28 Howell n.
Thlowe Elizabeth, 148 Manning n.
" Wm, " farmer.
Thomas Amy, 4 McCollum.
Thompson Frank, 49 Howell s, salesman.
" Celia, "
" Eugene, 78 Howell, painter.
Thurston Ella M, 36 Budlong, dressmkr.

Tw

Tibbetts D R, 205 Hillsdale, s.
" Elizabeth, 112 College e.
" Wm F, " col prof.
Tillottson Clarissa, 31 Manning n.
Timms Pearl, 43 Howell s.
Tinax Ann, 15 South w.
Todd Lucinda, Barnard.
" Margaret, 94 St Joseph.
" Martha, " domestic.
Tolford Flora, 19 Broad s, clerk.
Tolly Ametta A, 280 West n.
" Jas W, " college janitor.
" Isaac S, 261 Union n, wk in tan.
" Mary E, "
Townsend Claude, 181 West n, scn facty.
Traver Maud B, 36 Garden.
Travis Thos, 3 Howell, 'bus driver.
Tremains Andrew, 243 South e, peddler.
" Anna, "
" Elizabeth, "
" George A, " laborer.
" Jas F, " "
" John W, " "
Triechman Art, 57 Union, cooper.
" Fred, " "
" John, " laborer.
" John, Broad n, wk in livery.
" Maggie A, "
" Fred, 12 Waldron, cooper.
" Mary, "
Triplet Charles, 17 West s, carpenter.
" Josephine, "
Trostel Marilla, 94 West s, clerk.
Troy Millie, 50 Manning s, teacher.
Truax John, 272 Railroad e, laborer.
Tucker Grace, 21 Bacon e.
" John H, " train dispatchr.
Tunnington Kate, 53 Budlong.
" Frederick, " billiard room.
Turner Jeanette, 182 Hillsdale n.
Turrell Mary E, 111 Mead.
" Milton F, " postal clerk.
Tuttle Curtis, 46 Fayette e, laborer.
" Elizabeth, "
" Hudson, " drayman.
Twiss Alice, 74 Howell s.
Twiss Fred M., attorney at-law; City attorney for 1894; office, rooms 16 and 17 Waldron block; res 74 Howell s.
Twomley Celie, Bacon w.
" George A, " farmer.
" Melvin, "
" Anna S, 236 Park.

Wa

Twomley Frank M, 236 Park, huckster.
" George E, " barber.
" Minnie M, "
Tyler Adelia C, 94 Norwood ave.
" Alasko D, " farmer.
" George, " laborer.
" Ambrose C, Railroad w, farmer.
" Chas C, " clerk.
" Lemuel J, " s.
" Louise A, "
" Minnie, " teacher.
" Herbert, 31 Broad n, wk lunch r'm.
" Lottie, 62 Manning s, teacher.
Tyrrell Ollie I, 47 Howell s.
Underwood Jane B, 42 Manning n.
Updyke Henry, 234 Manning n, farmer.
" Phoebe J, "
" Syren, "
VanAllen, Eliza, 15 Oak.
" L H, " shoemaker.
VanAtta Bertha, 206 Manning n, s.
Vance George, 32 College e, s.
VanNess Charles, 202 Bacon e, laborer.
" Mary,
VanRiper Esther, 45 Budlong.
" Franklin, " machinist, (see Seney & VanRiper.)
VanValkenburgh Mollie, 81 River e, mus.
" Ebsom, 81 River e.
" Edith, " s.
" Eli, " horse trainer.
" Jessie, " teacher.
VanValkenberg Warren, Spring, laborer.
VanEvra Nicholas E, 63 West n, farmer.
VanMarter Emma, 52 Budlong.
VanWert Anna, 340 Hillsdale n.
VanWormer Abram, 58 West s, laborer.
Vaughn Myrtie, 13 Howder.
" Chas W, " r r conductor.
Vaughan S H, 191 Hillsdale, trav sales'n.
" C H, " s.
Veeder Chas. S., manufacturer of brooms, wholesale and retail; office 44 St Joseph e; res 34 Vine.
Veeder Edwin J, 34 Vine, broom maker.
" Mattie W, "
" Stella E, "
Vonsdeu Martha, 75 Bacon e, domestic.
Vreeland Jennie L, 63 Salem.
" Wm. " blacksmith.
Wade Herbert V, 306 West n, s.
Wagner Caroline, 8 Manning n.
" W A, 13 Howell s, sew mach opr.

We

Wagner Wm, 62 Waldron, trav salesman.
Wagor Minnie, Spring.
" Richard, 92 Hillsdale, plumber.
" Virginia M, "
" Wm, Spring, laborer.
Waldner Joseph, 81 St Joseph, laborer.
Waldner Maggie, 81 St Joseph.
Walker Eva M, 41 Budlong.
" Joseph, " teleg operator.
Waller Hattie B, 310 West n.
" Milo S, " s.
Walrath John J, 219 West n, carpenter.
" Lydia M, "
" Vinnie, " s.
Walters Ada, Bernard st.
Walters Isaac, 102 Broad n, laborer.
Walworth Fannie P, 30 Howell s.
" George E, " merchant.
" Joe, 102 Broad n, farmer.
" Lucien D, 2 Howell n, reg of deeds.
Ward Berton C, 62 State, r r fireman.
" Joseph S, 84 McCollum.
Ward Nellie E, 62 State, canvasser.
Warne Henry, 88 Hillsdale, carpenter.
" Libbie J, "
Warner Alvira A, 14 St Joseph.
" Andrew J, 41 West s, carpenter.
" Blake L, 14 St Joseph, laborer.
" Christie, 41 West s.
" Sarah M, 16 Mechanic.
Washburn Angeline, 108 State.
" Edwin M, " coal dealer.
" Emma E, 42 Howell s.
" George, " coal dealer.
" Oliver M, 108 State, s.
" Stella A, " s.
Watkins Francis M, colg bldg, minister.
" Jennie H, "
Watts Mary E, 98 Broad, domestic.
" Nora, " domestic.
Way Addie M, Bacon e.
" Emma, 21 Short.
" Fred H Short, work screen factory.
" Hiram L, 11 Short, vet. surgeon.
" Lewis, " carriage trimmer.
" Luther D, Bacon e, teleg ogerator.
" Mariah, 11 Short.
" Myron, 21 Short, engineer.
Weaver Chas B, 91 West n, r r scale insp.
" Charlotte, 228 West n.
" Flora E, 91 West n.
" Jas M, 219 Manning n, s.
Webb Marilla L, 67 Broad s.

Wh

Webber Charles, 188 Bacon e, miller.
" Clara, "
Weber Perry, Howell s, laborer.
Weeden Elizabeth, 12 Spring.
" Wm, " laborer.
Weir Emeline, 26 Budlong.
" Robert, " shoemaker.
" Kate, 38 Bacon w.
Welch Bridget, 64 Railroad w.
" Mary, "
" Harry T, 17 Champaign, laborer.
Wellman Amanda, 143 River e.
" Delmer E, " minister.
Wells Chas W, 2 Howell n, choreman.
" Frank P, 225 Hillsdale, s.
" Julius E, " s.
Werner Dr. J., Physician and Surgeon; office and res 61 Broad n.
Werner Matilda, 61 Broad n.
" Tilla, "
Westervelt Emma, 40 St Joseph.
" John, " cooper.
Westfall Eli, 90 Broad s, retired farmer.
" Esther, "
Weston Eliza, 132 Manning s.
" Lucius L, "
" Rose, 267 Bacon E, domestic.
Wheeler Carl W, 66 North, gas fitter.
" Edwin, 83 Mead, laborer.
" Frank, 40 Railroad e, carpenter.
" Jennie, 12 Ferris.
" Mary J, 40 Railroad e.
" Phoena V, 83 Mead.
" Sadie, 66 North.
Whipple James G, 186 Manning n, s.
" Louise, "
" Rosius, " postal clerk.
Whitcomb George A, 4 West n.
" Leonore B, "
White Clarence, 34 Howell s, trav sales.
" Commodore, 246 Bacon e, brick mas.
" John R, 102 Broad n, laborer.
" Levi, 24 Vine, carpenter.
" Lucinda, 246 Bacon e.
" Lucinda, 67 Manning n, domestic.
" May R, 24 Vine.
" Nellie, 34 Howell s.
" Wm, 246 Bacon e, bill poster.
Whitehead John H, 68 West n, clerk.
Whitlock Nora, 148 Manning n, domest.
Whitney Chas A, 88 Oak, carpenter.
" Chas W, 201 Hillsdale, s.
Whitbey Elizabeth, 88 Oak.

Wi

Whitney E. E., dealer in boots, shoes, gloves and mittens; 64 Howell n; res 88 Oak.
Whitney Fannie, 16 Bacon e.
" John, 44 Spring, r r fireman.
Whitney Dr. J. C., veterinary surgeon; treats diseases of all domesticated animals; office and residence 16 Bacon e.
Whitney Saphronia, 88 Oak.
Whittier Eliza, 22 Manning n.
Wichert Lewis G, 42 Union, pressman.
Widger Amanda, Baw Beese park.
Widger Norman N., Manager Baw Beese park.
Wilbur Burr, 33 West n, trav salesman.
" Fannie, 13 Manning n.
" Harriet, 33 West n.
" Ione, "
Wielander Jacob, 36 Hillsdale, lunch rm.
" Mary, "
Willard Libbie, 97 Howell s.
" Lou, " music teacher.
Wilder Nellie, 224 West n, s.
Williams Amanda, 66 St Joseph.
" Alexander, Norwood ave, laborer.
" Andrew, 19 Champaign, cooper.
" Chas, 114 Howder, laborer.
" Eleanor, 186 Hillsdale n, mus teach.
" Etta E, Bacon e.
" Henry, 66 St Joseph, teamster.
" John W, 43 Cemetery, cooper.
" John B, Bacon e, laborer.
" John H, 361 Hillsdale, laborer.
" Josephine, 361 Hillsdale.
" Julia, 64 Salem.
" Julia E, 99 Howder.
" Lottie, Norwood ave.
" Mattie, 43 Cemetery.
" Ruia, 114 Howder.
Williams S. N., proprietor tonsorial parlors in basement 56 Howell n; hair cutting, shaving, etc., artistically done; rasor honing and shear sharpening a specialty; res 99 Howder.
Willits Mary E, 33 North.
" Wm E, " merchant.
Wilmer Fred, 2 Howell n, hotel clerk.
Wilson Alice R, 7 Railroad.
" Floyd J, " painter.
" George, 70 North, peddler.
" Jennie, "
" Narida, 41 Manning s.

Wo

Winter Jay, 147 Howder, farmer.
" Nellie F, "
Winters Alovies, 85 Budlong, marb cutr.
" Margaret, "
" Mary, Hallet street.
" Peter, "
Winsor Ann C, 173 Hillsdale.
" Sarah, 92 Hillsdale.
Wiseman Adam, 79 Mead, tinner.
" Christina, "
" Conrad, 34 Cemetery, laborer.
" Peter, 27 Cemetery, r r laborer.
Wisil Andrew, 245 South e, painter.
" Carrie "
Withington Julia, 81 Howell s.
" Lauson, " clerk.
Withrow Edith M, 158 Hillsdale.
" John T, 158 Hillsdale, trav salesmn.
Wisner Clara J, 71 Railroad w, s.
" Julia A, "
" Margaret R, " dressmaker.
" Orin H, " laborer.
Wolcott Abbie A, Wolcott st.
" Abel, 3 Waldron.
" Burtis A, 45 Salem, s.
" Carrie L, 50 Howell s.
" Chas H, 45 Salem, broom maker.
Wolcott Chas. S., Photographer. The best photographs are made by Wolcott. 36 Howell st, 3rd floor; res 50 Howell s.
Wolcott Harriett, 3 Waldron.
" Julia A, 45 Salem.
" Mary A, "
" Nelson, Wolcott st, farmer.
Wolf Christina, 64 Bacon w.
" Christina, " book keeper.
" Geo C, "
" Geo P, " lumber dealer.
" John G, 60 Howell s, druggist.
" Lillian B, "
" Lizzie, 2 Howell n.
Wolfe Della S, 346 West n, s.
" John H, " s.
Wolven Albert, Hallet st.
" Christina, "
Wood Amy L, 83 West n, dressmaker.
" Elsie, 114 Hillsdale.
" Emma J, 85 Howder.
" Harriette I, 38 Garden.
" Hattie E, "
" Hattie, 114 Hillsdale.
" John M, 38 Garden, carpenter.
" Lillie E, 84 Howell.

Zi

Wood Marian A, 161 Manning n.
" Minnie, 294 West n.
" Myron G, 114 Hillsdale, farmer.
" Rachael, 85 Howder.
" Susan, 114 Hillsdale.
" Thomas A, 85 Howder, farmer.
" William, 84 Howell, merchant.
" Willie L, 38 Garden, r r employe.
" Wm R, 294 West n, minister.
" W W, 191 Hillsdale, s.
Woodruff Kate, 160 Manning n.
" Harriett A, "
" Sam S, " clerk.
" Walter, " painter.
" James P, 77 Broad s, clerk.
Woods Agnes, 42 Howell, teacher.
" Anne E, 224 Manning n, dressmukr.
Woodward Elijah M, 235 Union n, carp.
" Elizabeth A, "
Woodworth Frank, Bacon w, laborer.
" Laura A, 211½ Railroad.
" Otis J, " laborer.
" Park, 77 Broad.
Worthing Aaron, 113 Oak, (see Worthing & Alger)
" Edgar, 113 Oak.
" Lydia A, "
Worthing & Alger, proprietors of taunery, foot of Fayette street.
Wright Ella, 250 Bacon e.
" Mary, 158 Hillsdale, s.
" Zina, 250 Bacon e, brick mason.
" Wyatt Cornelia, 2 Howell n, pantry.
Wyckoff Ada, 2 Howell n, chambermaid.
Yates Charles H, 8 Spring, wk gas factry.
" Diamond, " "
" Permelia, "
" Smith, " farmer.
Yee Dong, 63 Broad, laundryman.
Yerfong, Yang " "
Young Clark N, 102 West n, mill wright.
Zackwriller Katie, 33 Broad s, domestic.
Zang Addie, 13 Manning s, clerk.
" Charlotte, "
Ziehr George, 25 Sharp, telegraph opr.
" " " shoemaker.
" Mary, "
Ziegler Henry, 237 South e, laborer.
" Mary, "

❋ Official Directory. ❋

Mayor—L. A. GOODRICH.
City Clerk—GEO. A. JANES.
Treasurer—ASHER B. LaFLEUR.
Collector and Ex-officio Marshal—WM. J. STONE.
Attorney—FRED M. TWISS.
Health Physician—E. E. MOORE.
Chief of Fire Dep't—WM. P. PERRY.

ALDERMEN.

First Ward, { Harry G. Bailey.
{ Edwin M. Washburn.
Second Ward, { Seth H. Smith.
{ Fay W. Elliott.
Third Ward, { Nathan M. Garrett.
{ Edwin C. Campbell.
Third Ward, { Chas. A. Shepard.
{ Ira Carpenter.

STANDING COMMITTEES.

Finance—BAILEY, SMITH, WASHBURN.
Streets—GARRETT, BAILEY, ELLIOTT.
Fire Department—
    SMITH, CAMPBELL, CARPENTER.
Public Works—
    WASHBURN, SMITH, GARRETT.
Supplies—SHEPARD, SMITH, CARPENTER.
Ordinances—
    CAMPBELL, BAILEY, WASHBURN.
Grievances—
    CARPENTER, ELLIOTT, SHEPARD.
Licenses—ELLIOTT, GARRETT, CAMPBELL.
Cemeteries—
    SHEPARD, ELLIOTT, CAMPBELL.
Sewers—GARRETT, WASHBURN, BAILEY.

BOARD OF EDUCATION.

Director—FRED H. STONE.
    CHAS. S. FRENCH.
    S. C. ROWLSON.
    C. W. TERWILLIGER.
    C. F. COOK.

GERMAN LUTHERAN CHURCH.
OFFICERS.
Steward—August Mœller.
Elder—Wm Emmert.
Trustees—George Oppel, Robert Seitz, J. Bachman.

YOUNG PEOPLE'S GERMAN SOCIETY.
(*Deutches Jugendbund.*)
President—Fred Seitz.

Vice President—Carrie Schmidt.
Secretary—Lizzie Alles.
Treasurer—Jas. McIntosh.
Entertainment Committee—Robert Seitz, Mrs. Jas. McIntosh, Mrs. H. Schafer, Miss Linda Spiegel.

ST. PETER'S EPISCOPAL.

Rector—(Vacancy.)
Senior warden—Geo. F. Gardner.
Junior warden—Robt. A. Weir.
Vestrymen — Jas. S. Galloway, H. B. Rowlson, Charles H. Smith, Guy M. Chester, John R. Sutton.

SUNDAY SCHOOL.
Superintendent—George F. Gardner.
Treasurer—Miss Frances Atwater.
Librarian—Pearl Timms.
Organist—Mrs. L. M. Lancaster.

ST. MARY'S GUILD.
President—Emma Prideaux.
Vice President—Bessie Ricaby.
Secretary—Frances Atwater.
Treasurer—Pearl Timms.

PRESBYTERIAN CHURCH.

BOARD OF TRUSTEES.
J. H. Armstrong, C. E. Eccles, C. H. Sheldon, Fred C. Thatcher, Dr. W. H. Sawyer.
Pastor—J. A. Crawford.
Ruling Elders — President, Dr. E. E. Moore; Allen Hammond, C. G. Robertson, F. D. Parmelee, W. Hughes, C. H. Sheldon, Allen Agnew, C. L. Thatcher.
Deacons — Rufus Campbell, Geo. A. Mark, E. A. Dibble, Stephen Betts.

PRESBYTERIAN SUNDAY SCHOOL.

Superintendent—C. H. Sheldon.
Assistant Superintendent—C. E. Eccles.
Secretary and Treasurer—Bertha Dibble.
Librarian—Richard A. Crippen.
Superintendent of Primary Department —Mrs. J. H. Ellis.

METHODIST EPISCOPAL CHURCH.

BOARD OF TRUSTEES.
S. H. Smith, O. W. Ferris, C. E. Singer. H. W. Gier, E. C. Bær, L. S. Ranney, R. O. Haynes.
Stewards—C. E. Singer, T. C. Montgomery, J. M. Clark, O. W. Ferris, G. M. Ruggles, Burt S. Alley, S. J. Gier,

Albert Stevens, W. L. Shuart, John Stone, F. W. Elliott, J. E. Fairbanks.

M. E. SUNDAY SCHOOL.

Superintendent—Samuel J. Gier.
Assistant Superintendent—C. E. Singer.
Secretary—Bert S. Ally.
Treasurer—J. M. Clark.
Librarian—O. W. Ferris.
Superintendent of Primary Department —Belle Stimson.

FREEWILL BAPTIST CHURCH.

Millie Mead, clerk.
Dilla Allis, assistant clerk.
A. Worthing, treasurer.
Deacons—C. H. Sayles, A. Worthing, K. Batchelder, H. Cook, S. B. Dyer.
Trustees—A. Worthing, E. M. Washburn, K. Batchelder, C. H. Sayles, C. S. Hayes, Mrs. J. L. Copp, Mrs. S. B. Randolph, G. W. Myers, Dr. C. C. Johnson.

FIRST BAPTIST CHURCH.
BOARD OF TRUSTEES.

Pastor—E. M. Griffin.
F. H. Conklin, F. M. Stewart, A. B. Prentice, E. J. Estey, Geo Ferris, Job Cole, jr., Malcolm Dow, O. H. Risedorph, H. B. Granger.
Clerk—Ella Guy.
Treasurer—F. H. Conklin.

BAPTIST SUNDAY SCHOOL.

Superintendent—Ray Blakeman.
Sec. and Treas.—Harry McClave.
Librarian—Sadie Stafford.

❋ **Society Directory.** ❋

EUREKA COMMANDERY, NO. 3, KNIGHT TEMPLAR.

Eminent Commander—E. T. Beckhardt.
Generalissimo—M. E. Hall.
Captain-General—G. M. Chester.
Prelate—L. S. Ranney.
Senior Warden—Geo. J. Kline.
Junior Warden—F. H. Stone.
Treasurer—J. H. Armstrong.
Recorder—Morris Lamb.
Standard Bearer—Chas. Homan.
Sword Bearer—W. H. Tallman.

Warder—W. H. Frankhauser.
Sentinel—J. C. Heenan.
Guards—W. R. Branch, H. P. Mead and Geo. B. Gardner.

MT. ARARAT COUNCIL, NO. 15, R. & S. M.

T. I. M.—Ira Carpenter.
D. M.—F. J. Wilson.
P. C. W.—J. H. Ellis.
Treasurer—J. H. Armstrong.
Recorder—L. S. Ranney.
C. of G.—L. H. Frensdorf.
C. of C.—H. W. Samm.
Steward—R. Hoffman.
Sentinel—Jas. McIntosh.

HILLSDALE CHAPTER NO. 18, R. A. M.

H. P.—G. M. Chester.
K.—Geo. M. Drummond.
S.—J. H. Ellis.
C. of H.—W. H. Frankhauser.
P. S.—E. I. Frankhauser.
R. A. C.—Geo. J. Kline.
M. 3d V.—Irving Dean.
M. 2d V.—Albert Gould.
M. 1st. V.—Jas. McKee.
Treasurer—C. E. Lawrence.
Secretary—Sam Woodruff.
Sentinel—Jas. McIntosh.
Stewards—H. W. Samm and H. P. Mead.

HILLSDALE LODGE, NO. 176, F. & A. M.

W. M.—E. I. Frankhauser.
Senior Warden—W. H. Frankhauser.
Junior Warden—Fred M. Twiss.
Treasurer—Chas. S. French.
Secretary—W. P. Perry.
Senior Deacon—W. H. French.
Junior Deacon—C. W. Jones.
Stewards—W. A. Wagner and Henry Wilson.
Chaplain—Sam J. Gier.
Tiler—Frank Proctor.
Trustees—(Vacant.)

FIDELITY LODGE, NO. 32, F. & A. M.

W. W.—J. H. Ellis.
S. W.—J. W. McKee.
J. M.—E. E. Moore.
S. D.—H. C. Blackman.
J. D.—F. O. Hancock.
Secretary—F. J. Wilson.
Treasurer—J. H. Armstrong.
Tiler—Wm. Plum.
Stewards—F. L. Greene and F. J. Gray.

Trustees—Jas. S. Galloway and L. S. Ranney.

HILLSDALE LODGE NO. 17, I. O. O. F.

N. G.—D. M. Gillett.
V. G.—(Vacant)
Recording Secretary—A. Holdridge.
Permanent Secretary—J. E. Porter.
Treasurer—M. W. Taylor.

TREADWAY ENCAMPMENT NO. 9.

C. P.—M. Selles.
S. W.—H. H. Frankenfield.
J. W.—R. A. Lester.
Scribe—J. E. Porter.
Treasurer—O. A. Janes.

CRYSTAL LODGE NO. 9, DAUGHTERS OF REBECCA.

Noble Grand—Mrs. D. M. Gillett.
Vice Grand—Mrs. Castle.
Recording Secretary—(Vacant)
Treasurer—Mrs. Wellington Hughes.
Financial Secretary—Mrs. Julia Taylor.
Chaplain—Mrs. H. H. Frankenfield.
Warden—Mrs. O. Riggs.
Conductor—Mrs. F. Dush.

ROYAL ARCANUM COUNCIL NO. 168.

Regent—C. H. Sheldon.
Secretary—Geo. F. Gardner.
Treasurer—Dr. R. A. Everett.
Collector—C. L. Budd.

CANTON HILLSDALE NO. 16.

Captain—A. H. English.
Lieutenant—F. M. Stanton.
Ensign—James Flint.
Colonel—E. E. Holdridge.
Accountant—Wm. T. Seidel.

C. J. DICKERSON POST, G. A. R. NO. 6.

Commander—Geo. E. Porter.
S. V. C.—V. Riggs.
J. V. C.—Chas. H. Fairbanks.
Surgeon—Dr. R. A. Everett.
Chaplain—D. F. Austin.
Quartermaster—A. H. English.
Adjutant—W. H. Tallman.
O. D.—W. M. Taylor.

GEO. W. LUMBARD CAMP, NO. 5, S. OF V., DIVISION OF MICHIGAN.

Captain—S. B. Marble.
First Lieut.—H. E. Chatfield.
Second Lieut.—Rollo Dailey.
First Sergeant—O. J. Riggs.

Quartermaster Sergeant—W. H. Green.
Chaplain—Fred M. Twiss.
Sergeant of the Guard—S. A. Foquer.
Corporal of the Guard—Theodore Taylor.
Musician—E. P. S. Miller.
Color Sergeant—C. E. Triplett.
Camp Guard—J. G. Dailey.
Picket Guard—Herbert Higbee.

C. J. DICKERSON W. R. C., NO. 37.

President—Julia M. Taylor.
S. V. P.—Mary Locklin.
J. V. P.—Anna Nimocks.
Secretary—Louise Whipple.
Treasurer—Carrie Perry.
Chaplain—Melissa Crum.
Conductor—Adaline Croose.
Guard—Ellen Smith.
Assistant Guard—Cordelia McClave.
Assistant Conductor—Hattie Riker.

A. F. WHELAN COMMAND NO. 31, UNION VETERANS' UNION.

Colonel—H. V. D. Baker.
Lieutenant-Colonel—V. Riggs.
Major—D. H. Briggs.
Adjutant—O. A. Janes.
Quartermaster—G. A. Riker.
Surgeon—H. Fellows.
Chaplain—W. Lathrop.
Officer of Day—G. B. Shaffer.
Officer of Guard—A. Wolvin.

HILLSDALE LODGE, NO. 45, K. OF P.

C. C.—A. L. Guernsey.
V. C.—A. Cory.
Prelate—H. Shaffer.
M. of Work—L. B. Dickinson.
K. of R. & S.—Fred Perry.
M. of F.—A. W. Brooks.
M. of E.—James McIntosh.
M. at A.—H. H. Frankenfield.
Outside Guard—D. M. Gillett.
Inside Guard—F. Speer.
Trustees—L. A. Goodrich and O. A. Janes.
Representative—W. P. Perry.
Installing Officer—O. A. Janes.

HILLSDALE TENT NO. 181, K. O. T. M.

Past Commander—Eli Hughes.
Commander—E. L. Baxter.
Lieut-Commander—O. A. Janes.
Record Keeper—L. H. McClave.
Finance Keeper—W. J. Stone.
Prelate—E. B. Marsh.

Kochenthal Bros. & Co., Leading Clothiers, Furnishers & Hatters.

Physician--W. H. Sawyer.
Sergeant--A. U. Brooks.
Master-at-Arms--Wesley Steward.
First Master-of-guards--W. H. Peterson.
Second Master-of-guards-W.L.VanDusen
Sentinel--Wm. Johnson.
Picket--Frank K. Dillon.

EQUITABLE AID UNION.

Chancellor--L. L. Locklin.
President--H. H. Frankenfield.
Vice-President--D. M. Gillett.
Advocate--M. H. Davis.
Auxilliary--Mrs. A. Wolcott.
Chaplain--(Vacant)
Secretary--Mrs. H. H. Frankenfield.
Accountant and Treas.--W. J. Sampson.
Conductor--Mrs. D. M. Gillett.
Assistant Conductor--Mrs. Emma Cole.
Warden--Mrs. Addie Croose.
Outside Watchman--N. Young.
Inside Watchman--R. A. Lester.

HATHAWAY LODGE, NO. 130, ORDER OF ÆGIS.

Past President--Herbert Knapp.
President--Geo. L. Hathaway.
Vice-President--Miss Nellie Wheeler.
Secretary--Mrs. Virginia Wagor.

Treasurer--Will VanDusen.
Chaplain--Miss Eva Hyde.
Medical Examiner--Dr. W. H. Sawyer.
Marshal--Mrs. Adaline Croose.
Guard--Miss Maud Hyde.
Sentinel--Will Ransier.
Trustees--Frank Wheeler, Geo. Van-
Dusen, Richard Wagor.

LADIES' BENEVOLENT SOCIETY.

President--Mrs. F. W. Stock.
Vice-president--Mrs. Justin Gray.
Secretary--Mrs. Geo. Harding.
Treasurer--Mrs. A. D. Stock.

LADIES' LIBRARY ASSOCIATION.

President--Mrs. M. McIntyre.
Vice-president--Mrs. I. T. Bryan.
Secretary--Mrs. S. D. Bishopp.
Treasurer--Mrs. Wm. Cook.
Librarian--Miss Kate Russell.
Sutton block; open Saturday afternoon 3 to 6 o'clock summers and 2 to 5 o'clock from October 1 to May 1.

W. C. T. U.

President--Mrs. J. R. Mowry.
Treasurer--Addie Prentiss.
Secretary--Mrs. D. B. Reed.

A CLASSIFIED LIST

Of the Business Firms and Business Men of Hillsdale.

BANKS AND BANKERS.

THE FIRST NATIONAL BANK OF HILLSDALE: The oldest National Bank in Southern Michigan. See card, page 42.

DRY GOODS.

BOYLE & BROWN: Dry goods merchants; this firm established itself in business in Hillsdale in 1890. It enjoys a large trade, both from the city and country. They keep an attractive store, obliging salesmen and an A1 stock. See foot ads bottom of page.

GEO. J. KLINE & Co.: This is another firm that ranks high in the trade. It first began doing business in 1884. A complete assortment of dry goods is always on hand. The store always presents a neat and tasty appearance and customers are always sure of the best of attention and bargains.

CLOTHING, GENTS' FURNISHERS AND MERCHANT TAILORS.

L. GUGGENHEIM: The oldest clothing merchant in the city, established in 1857. Besides handling a full line of clothing and gents' furnishing a merchant tailoring department is conducted. See card, page 44.

KOCHENTHAL BROS. & Co.: This is perhaps the most popular firm in the clothing trade in Hillsdale. They keep a complete and stylish line of clothing and gents' furnishings and lead in the merchant tailoring business. See ads. top of pages and covers.

L. FRENSDORF: The hatter and gents' furnisher, keeps the best line of goods in the city in the way of hats and gents' furnishings. This concern was established in 1877 and has the leading trade in the city in the way of stylish and latest furnishings for gentlemen. This firm has the exclusive agency for the celebrated Dunlap hats. See ad. on map.

HOTELS, RESTAURANTS AND BOARDING HOUSES.

KEEFER HOUSE: Chas. E. Keefer, proprietor. Erected in 1885. One of the two best hotels in the city. Improvements such as steam heat free, electric light, etc. Rates per day are $2.00. See ad.

SMITH'S HOTEL: A. B. Dickinson, proprietor. This building was erected in 1874 by Smith Bros.; the management fell into Mr. Dickinson's hands in 1876. It is one of the two best hotels in the city. Rates are $2.00 per day. All appointments are first class and modern. See adv.

GILLETT'S HOTEL: Daniel Gillett, proprietor. This is a good respectable house for the traveling public; everything arranged for the convenience of patrons. Rates are $3.50 to $4.00 per week, day rates $1.00. See card, page 44.

COTTAGE HOTEL: Return P. Hawes, proprietor; this house enjoys a rushing business the year around; it is a neat comfortable place, both for transients and weekly boarders. Rates are $3.50 to $4.00 per week, day rates $1.00. See card, page 45.

KAHLER HOUSE: John Kahler, proprietor. One of the most accommodating places in the city; the traveling public and others are assurred of courteous treatment at the Kahler house. Rates per week $3.50, $1.00 per day. See card, page 47.

PHYSICIANS.

F. M. GIER, M. D.: Established here in 1890; graduate of University of Michigan, class of '84, regular department; secretary of board of pension examiners; president Tri-state Medical Association. See card, page 43.

WALTER H. SAWYER, M. D.: Established in 1884; graduate of University of Michigan, regular department. See card, page 56.

ELI HUGHES, M. D.: Began practice here in 1885; graduate of Bellevue Medical college, New York city. See card, page 47.

E. E. MOORE, M. D.: Began practice here in 1884; graduate of Dartmouth Medical college and New York Post-graduate colleges. See card, page 51.

H. H. HARRIS, M. D.: Established here in 1873; graduate of Northwestern university, class of '72. See card, page 45.

J. WERNER, M. D.: Established here in 1873; graduate of Detroit Medical college. See card, page 62.

GROCERS, FLOUR AND FEED.

E. L. RANNEY: This firm carries a well selected stock of groceries and since going into business, fall of '93, have gained control of a large patronage; flour and feed are also carried along with the regular grocery line. See card, page —.

O. HANCOCK: Proprietor of grocery store began business in 1866; this store is equipped with a well selected grocery stock and does as large a business in this line as any other in town. See card, page 45.

GEO. W. MEYERS: Proprietor of the "Variety store" on College Hill; established in this place in 1891; a well kept stock of groceries and a small line of stationery comprises the outfit. See card, page 52.

T. M. FANT: Proprietor of one of the largest groceries in the city; a fancy stock of groceries and table luxuries are always kept; established in 1886; this is one of the leading firms in the place. See card, page 41.

LEVI H. CORSON: Recently established in business. He has a well selected stock of groceries and provisions and has a good trade. See card under Corrections and Additions.

L. F. COLE: Proprietor grocery store; established in 1891; this firm is well known as a leading grocery exchange and has a well earned patronage; the best in the line is handled and none other. See card under Corrections and Additions.

J. GRAY: An old-time grocer established here in 1872; he is now conducting a finely equipped grocery on Broad street, north. See card, page 54.

E. J. SMITH: Conducts one of the best groceries in the city; established here in 1880. See card, page 57.

JEWELERS.

M. V. B. ROWLEY: See card, page 55.

C. L. BUDD: See card, page 36.

ALBAUGH & SON: See card, page 33.

REAL ESTATE, INSURANCE.

L. P. REYNOLDS: Established in the real estate business in 1872; nothing but the best of insurance companies are represented. See card, page 54.

JOHN R. SUTTON: Established in business in 1890; a long list of substantial companies is represented; besides insurance a loan business is conducted. See card, page 60.

JULIAN A. PALMER: Real estate agency; farms and other property bought and sold and exchanged. See card, page 53.

DRUGGISTS AND PHARMACISTS.

CHAS. S. FRENCH: Proprietor of drug store; conducts one of the best equipped stores in the city; in the drug line there is a complete stock; a prescription department is under careful management; the usual side lines such as perfumes, cigars, soda water and other summer drinks are also kept in stock. Established, 1860. See ad. on top of pages.

L. A. GOODRICH & Co.: This firm began business in 1837; it has worked up a large trade since that time; is one of the leading drug firms of the place; the regular complete stock of drugs together with a well assorted line of perfumes, cigars, etc., is carried. See card, page 44.

BOOKS, STATIONERY AND NEWS DEPOT.

C. L. THATCHER & SON: This firm was established in 1890. It has the exclusive stationery and book trade in the city; aside from the regular stock of books and stationery, musical merchandise and wall paper are carried. See card, page 60.

BOOTS AND SHOES.

C. H. SHELDON: This is one of the leading shoe firms in the city; everything is kept to make up a complete stock of leather and rubber goods; besides these is a stock, full line, of gloves and mittens; the lowest of living prices prevail and a large and steady trade is the result. See card.

E. E. WHITNEY: Proprietor of shoe store; a complete stock of leather and rubber goods always on hand; mittens and gloves are also kept in stock; established in 1888.

MEAT MARKETS.

J. W. LAMBERT: Proprietor of meat market, began business here in 1863; a fresh line of meats, fish and vegetables are handled. See card, page 49.

W. H. CROOSE & Co.: This is one of the largest firms in the city in this line; established in 1889; a complete line of meats, fish and vegetables in season. See card under Corrections and Additions.

HARDWARE, BICYCLES AND SPORTING GOODS.

GEO. F. GARDNER: Proprietor of hardware store; this firm deals in a general stock of hardware and bicycles; established in 1870; it has continued to prosper and at present has a large list of customers. See card, page —.

C. E. LAWRENCE & Co.: Hardware firm; one of the leading houses in the city; general stock of hardware, bicycles and sporting goods; established in 1872. See card, page 49.

GEO. N. SMITH: The firm began business in 1890; a complete line in general hardware is handled; aside from this is a line of bicycles and sporting goods which cannot be excelled by any others in the city.

LAWYERS.

FRANK A. LYON: Began practice here in 1891. See card under Corrections and Additions.

Frankhauser Bros.: Firm established in 1891. See card, page 43.

S. D. Bishopp: Began practice here in 1876. See card, page 35.

Guy M. Chester: Began practice here in 1886. See card, page 37.

Fred M. Twiss: Began practice of law in 1891. See card, page 60.

James T. Chestnut: Established here in 1889. See card, page 37.

W. C. Chadwick: Established here in 1888; graduate of University of Michigan, class '87. See card, page 37.

Fred. H. Stone: Established here in 1878; studied with St. John & Dickerman. See card, page 59.

W. J. Sampson: Established here in 1889; studied in Marcellus, Cass county. See card, page 56.

A. L. Guernsey: Established here in 1887; studied with Weaver & Shepard. See card, page 44.

Delmer E. Fast: Established here in 1880; studied with Judge D. L. Pratt. See card under Corrections and Additions.

Bailey & Janes: Established in 1889. See card under Corrections and Additions.

Geo. F. Knickerbocker: Established in 1855. See card, page 48.

Sylvester L. Dwight: Established here in 1886; graduate of University of Michigan, class of '67. See card, page 41.

W. R. Montgomery: Established in 1859. See card, page 51.

M. McIntyre: Established in practice of law, 1875. See card, page —.

CROCKERY AND GLASSWARE.

H. P. Mead & Co.: Dealers in crockery and glassware; established in 1879; a large and varied stock is carried by this firm the year around; it is the only store of its kind in the city and the firm enjoys an exclusive trade in this line. See ad.

COOPERAGE WORKS.

L. Globensky: Proprietor of cooperage works; this plant turns out annually 10,000 barrels; fifteen to twenty men are employed; Mr. Globensky commenced in business here in 1894; it is one of the solid manufacturing concerns of the place and gives employment to its men steadily the entire year.

MARBLE DEALERS.

G. M. Ruggles: Proprietor of the Hillsdale Marble Works; established in 1882; employment furnished to five men the entire year. See card, page 55.

FREDONIA WASHER COMPANY.

J. S. Parker: Manufacturer of the celebrated Fredonia Washer; one of the handiest articles ever invented for washing purposes; office on Broad street, north. See card under Corrections and Additions.

WHOLESALE GROCER.

Lane & Co.: This firm was established in 1888. It supplies the several retail grocery firms about the city and county with articles of trade. See card, page 49.

VETERINARY SURGEONS.

J. C. Whitney: See card and ad.

E. C. Delavan: See card under Corrections and Additions.

MUSIC DEALERS.

A. Cory: See card under Corrections and Additions.

LIVERIES AND HACK LINES.

HINKLE BROS.: See card, page 46.
SMITH BROS.: See card, page 58.
A. T. PETERSON: See card under Corrections and Additions.

DENTIST.

DR. F. E. MOREY: See card, page 51.

PHOTOGRAPHERS.

W. B. BOUTWELL: See card and ad.
CHAS. S. WOLCOTT: See card and ad.

AGRICULTURAL IMPLEMENTS.

HILLSDALE TRANSFER CO.: J. F. Fitzsimmons, manager; office and warehouse corner Welch and East Railroad street.

FURNITURE AND UNDERTAKING.

FERRIS & SINGER: See ad. bottom pages.

LUMBER DEALERS.

GEO. P. WOLF: Dealer in lumber. See card under Corrections and Additions.

COAL, WOOD AND ICE.

E. H. CUNNINGHAM: See card, page 39,

BROOM MANUFACTURERS.

CHAS. S. VEEDER: See card, page 61.

FOUNDRY AND MACHINE SHOP.

SENEY & VAN RIPER: See card, page 57.

MILLINER AND DRESSMAKER.

MISS IRENE CARPENTER: Milliner. See card and ad.
MISS JETTIE MALONEY: Modiste. See card, page 50.

SEWING MACHINE AGENTS.

H. C. BAKER: See card under Corrections and Additions.
WM. KITCHEN: See card, page 48.

CIGAR MANUFACTURERS.

HILLSDALE CIGAR CO.: Established 1898; employs fifteen hands. See card, page 46.

TANNERY.

WORTHING & ALGER: Proprietors of tannery. See card, page 63.

TONSORIAL ARTISTS.

S. M WILLIAMS: See card, page 62.
FRED ENGELHARDT: See card, page 41.
LEON HATHAWAY: See card, page 45.

LAUNDRY.

MRS. H. P. BAIL: Proprietor of Hillsdale Steam Laundry. See card, page 49

GERMAN LUTHERAN CHURCH.

At Chas S. French's, ❋ ❋

(Three Doors North of Smith's Hotel)

You will find a Very Complete
Stock of Pure Drugs and Medicines.

―――――

CHOICE FAMILY GROCERIES,
KEY WEST and DOMESTIC CIGARS,
PERFUMES and TOILET REQUISITES,
PURE WINES and LIQUORS for Medicinal Use,
PATENT and PROPRIETARY MEDICINES,
TABLETS, PENS and PAPETERIES,
PAINTS, OILS and WALL PAPER.
THE MOST DELICIOUS ICE CREAM and SODA WATER
AND ALL ARTICLES USUALLY SOLD AT A
FIRST CLASS DRUG STORE.

―――――

RECIPES AND PRESCRIPTIONS CAREFULLY COMPOUNDED BY
EXPERIENCED PHARMACISTS, FROM THE PUREST MATERIALS, AND
AT REASONABLE PRICES.

CHAS. S. FRENCH.

www.ingramcontent.com/pod-product-compliance
Lightning Source LLC
Chambersburg PA
CBHW030000030726
47499CB00008B/2828